Stranded
at Sheep Camp

Karen Glinski

Stranded

ISBN: 978-0615936895
Library of Congress Control Number: 2014939113

Cover and interior art (pages 43, 47, 77, 177): Debbie Jennings Fowler
Chapter icons and additional interior art (page 130): Daina Heeter
Cover and interior design: Anne Flanagan
Author photographs: Kim Jew Photography (author photo)
Photo back cover (sheep): Ookaboo
Type is set in Times Roman.
Contact the author at glinskikaren@gmail.com.

NIGHTHAWK PRESS
TAOS, NEW MEXICO

DEDICATION

This book is dedicated to young people of all ages from every culture and country. Coping with unwanted changes in life can be overwhelming, and developing the courage to deal with them can be the biggest challenge of all.

ACKNOWLEDGMENTS

Joan Leslie Woodruff for your faith in my story and my ability to write it. Thank you for your belief in me and for editing at least three versions, including the final one.

Sandy Schauer for your encouragement and persistence in helping me become a better writer. Thank you for your belief in me and for editing the final version.

Los Lunas critique group members for your support, professionalism, good humor, occasional finger-wagging and sincere friendship: Sandy Schauer, Laura Sanchez, Helen Pilz and Lisa Garcia. I could not have written this book without you.

Albuquerque critique group members for all the reasons noted above: Kathy Richter-Sand, Evee Moore, Sabrina Strong and Desiree Perriguey.

Esther Yazzie-Lewis for your Navajo 101 class where you patiently taught me correct pronunciation of so many beautiful Navajo words, for your delightful humor and for editing the final version of my story.

CONTENTS

GLOSSARY OF NAVAJO AND SPANISH WORDS

Aoo. Means "yes." Pronounced "Oh."

Bighan. Means "home" or "corral." Pronounced "Bih-gone."

Bilagaana. Means "White man" or can refer to White man's culture. Pronounced "bih-la-gana."

Cheii. Means "maternal grandfather." Pronounced "Chay" as in Jay.

Ch'iidii. Means "devil" or "evil spirits." Pronounced "Chee-dee."

Dibe. Means "sheep." Pronounced "dih-bay."

Diné. Means "Navajo." Pronounced "Dih-nay."

Dooda. Means "no." Pronounced "Do-dah."

Gah. Means "rabbit." Pronounced "gah."

Hagonnee. Means "good-bye." Pronounced "ha-go-nay."

Hogan. Means "house or home or dwelling." Pronounced "ho-gone."

Hosteen. Means a term of respect given to elder Navajo men. Pronounced "ho-steen."

Kin. Means "store or building." Pronounced "kin."

Ma'ii. Means "coyote." Pronounced "mah-eee"

Mesa. Means "table" and refers to the seemingly flat expanse of land at high altitude. Pronounced "may-sah."

Nahashch'id. Means "badger hunter." Pronounced "na-hash-chid."

Shi. Means "my." Pronounced "shih."

T'aa'akodi. Means "the end" or "that's all." Pronounced "tah-a-ko-dih."

Tsoi. Means "maternal grandson." Pronounced "tsoy."

Ti'izi. Means "goat." Pronounced "tli-tsee."

Ya'at'eeh. Means "hello." Pronounced "ya-ah-te."

1

The Best Summer Ever

"Gotcha!" Emerson whooped and pumped both fists in the air. *Call of Duty: Black Ops* was his favorite video game, and he was pretty good at it. He turned to his friend. "Let's go again, Zach. You might even win, if you're lucky." Emerson settled back in his chair, feeling smug.

Zach punched the remote and the video screen went dark. "We're done with fifth grade. It's summer vacation! We can play video games anytime. Let's plan other things to do."

Emerson pushed his glasses to the bridge of his nose. All year long he'd thought about what to do when summer arrived. "I've got some ideas. Remember that place, Stone Age Climbing Gym, where we climbed up fake cliffs?"

"Totally! That's awesome. Okay, how about laser

tag at Hinkle Fun Center?"

"Yeah, we can do that again." Emerson played it once before with Zach but got tagged a lot. *If I play long enough, I'll get so good that I'll do all the tagging.* "And Isotopes games. Our parents might come because they like baseball. But we don't have to sit with them."

Zach nodded. "Hey, how about BMX track? We always wanted to watch the bike races."

"I thought of that, too!" Emerson paused for a moment. "You know, if our parents let us do this stuff, they'll make us do something educational, too."

"You're right." Zach stared at the ceiling. "We better think of something before they do."

"I got it! The Rattlesnake Museum." Emerson laughed, pleased with his brilliance. "We've got lots of rattlers here in Albuquerque. We should learn about them."

Zach grinned. "I hear some of the exhibits really creep you out."

Emerson high-fived his friend. "This'll be the best summer ever!"

Suddenly, *Star Wars* music belted from a cell phone. Emerson jumped. "Mom let me use her cell today. I asked for one of my own, but Dad said no. I don't get it. Everyone else has one." He punched the green button. "Yeah, Mom?"

His mother's voice sounded small and far away. "Honey, I know you're hanging out with Zachary, but I

2

want you to come home."

"Right now?" His shoulders slumped. "I just got here."

"Yes, Emerson. Now." Her voice trailed off. "Something's come up."

Emerson rolled his eyes at Zach. "Ohh-kay. I'll be home in a few minutes."

He punched the off button and shoved the phone back inside his pocket. "Mom sure sounds strange. Like something's wrong."

"What did you do now?"

"Nothing."

"Your mom and dad been fighting?"

"Don't think so. At least not when I'm around. But they're both acting weird." Emerson chewed on his lower lip. "They've been acting weird for a while."

Zach opened a box of Milk Duds and poured some into his hand. "Here," he tossed the box to Emerson. "Parents. Who can understand them?"

"Not me." Emerson popped a Milk Dud in his mouth. "Last night I heard Dad ask Mom if she was ready for her classes. She said not really."

Zach gestured for the candy box. "That's right. Your mom's starting college. She wants to be a nurse, right?"

"Yeah," Emerson said. "Maybe that's it. Dad said things would change when Mom goes back to school."

"Yeah. See? It's not you, after all."

Emerson got up. "Better get going. See ya." He

3

headed down the hall and opened the front door.

"Later," Zach yelled from his room.

Emerson rode his bike two blocks to his house. Traffic on Kirtland Air Force Base was slow in the housing area, and he daydreamed while he rode. Turning the corner, he saw his Dad's Honda scooter parked outside the garage.

He checked his watch. *Four o'clock. Why isn't he at work? He's never home this early.* Emerson began to feel uneasy. *Mom said something came up, and her voice didn't sound right.* Emerson coasted into the driveway and leaned his bike against the garage door.

He heard them talking when he walked inside.

"We're in the kitchen, Son," Dad called out.

Rounding the corner, Emerson found them sitting at the kitchen table with cups of coffee. A can of Coca-Cola sat at his place. He slid into his chair, popped the top and took a gulp. Something was definitely wrong if they had a Coke waiting for him.

His father leaned forward. "We have something to tell you. Your mother has known for almost a month now. Things will be different for a while, actually, for a year. The Air Force gave me a new job."

"A new job?" Emerson leaned back in his chair. "Why? What's wrong with your old one?" He looked back and forth from mom to dad. Neither one looked happy, and his stomach began to churn.

His father smiled. "Nothing's wrong with my old one. My commanding officer is proud of the work I do."

"So why are you guys acting weird? What's going on?"

"Emerson, your mother and I decided to wait until school was out before telling you. We didn't want to interfere with your classes or your final tests."

Emerson clenched his fists. "What is it, Dad? Just tell me!"

Mom reached over and rubbed Emerson's shoulder. "Emerson, the Air Force is transferring your dad to another base."

"We have to move again? No!" Emerson jerked away. "I don't want to. I made friends here."

"No, Son. You and your mother won't move. Only me. I'm being deployed to Afghanistan. I leave the day after tomorrow."

2
My Summer's Ruined

Emerson felt like someone slammed him with a soccer ball. "What? You're going to Afghanistan? For a year?"

His father nodded. "Your mother and I have been busy working out the details. That's probably why you thought we were acting weird. The military requires families to be prepared when a parent is deployed."

"Why do YOU have to go? Why can't they pick someone else's dad?"

"Emerson, they picked me because of the job I do. I have no choice. You're old enough to remember the last three times we moved. I had no choice then, either."

"Yeah, but we all moved together." Emerson chugged some Coke. His brain felt empty, like there were questions he should ask but couldn't think of. He looked at Mom. "What'll we do while Dad's gone?"

"Well, honey, some of it you already know. I start nursing school Monday. I'll work part-time at Lovelace Hospital when I'm not in school." She was quiet for a moment. "I won't be home much. I'll be very, very busy."

"So what about me? Zach and I made lots of summer plans. I guess his mom could drive us around. We're going to climb cliffs and watch the BMX bike races and — "

"Emerson, stop," Dad interrupted.

Emerson's insides began to churn again. *Something's really wrong with Dad's voice.*

"Dad," he began again slowly. "What about me?"

Dad glanced over at Mom and reached for her hand. "Son, your mom will be at work or school all day, every day except Sunday. When she comes home, she'll have to study. She won't have time to take care of you."

"That's okay!" Emerson turned to his mother. "Mom, I'm old enough to take care of myself. Zach's mom and dad would let me spend time at their house. And I can help you with your homework. I get really good grades."

"No, honey," Mom shook her head. "It's already been decided. You'll spend the summer with your grandfather."

Emerson slumped back in his chair. At first, he couldn't speak. "Aren't Grandpa and Grandma somewhere in South America?"

8

"No," Dad said. "Grandma and Grandpa Wright are doing missionary work in Guatemala. That's Central America, but they can't take care of you, either."

Emerson felt confused. "Then what grandfather are you talking about?"

Mom leaned forward. "Grandpa Charlie. You remember. He visited us when we first moved to Albuquerque. He's Navajo, like me, and — "

"No!" Emerson pushed back his chair. "I remember him now. He and Dad yelled at each other, and it made you cry. Then he left. I never want to see him again."

"Honey, I know that's a bad memory, but he was a good father to me. He'll be a good grandfather to you."

"If he's so good, why can't he come here and stay with us?"

Mom shook her head. "Emerson, it's not that simple. He has a whole herd of sheep to care for. He can't just drop everything and come here."

"But you want ME to drop everything and go there!" He jumped up and glared at his mother. "That's not fair! You don't care what I want! You just want to get rid of me!"

Emerson stomped out of the kitchen and toward the front door. He heard Dad say, "Let him go. We should have told him sooner." Emerson yanked open the door and slammed it behind him.

Outside, he stopped a moment and caught his breath. Then he pushed the kickstand on his bike and pedaled off down the street. His thoughts tumbled around in his head. *I can't believe it! They treat me like a little kid. I hate that. My summer's ruined! I don't want to go to wherever that grandfather lives. It's just not fair!* Turning onto Zach's street, Emerson saw his friend with Tim, another guy from class.

Emerson hit his brakes and skidded to a stop next to the curb.

"Hey!" Zach said. "We're going to Tim's house. Want to come?"

"I don't know. I just heard my dad's going to Afghanistan."

"Whoa. Afghanistan? When?"

"Sunday. THIS Sunday. Like the day after tomorrow Sunday."

"Afghanistan, huh?" Tim stepped closer. "Remember Gloria? Her dad went there right after school started. He got killed. I remember she cried a lot."

"Yeah," Zach said. "But Jeff's mom came back, remember? She went to Iraq, didn't she? Maybe Iraq's where your dad should go, not Afghanistan."

"He can't choose. He has to go where the Air Force sends him. We know that."

"Well, maybe Jeff's mom got lucky," Tim said. "They blow up lots of trucks and people in Iraq. It's always on the news – body parts everywhere. I bet that happens in Afghanistan, too."

Emerson clenched his teeth. "Stop it! I don't want

to talk about it." He glared at his friends, feeling a big lump grow in his throat.

"Sorry," Zach said. "I guess it's different if it's your dad's body parts."

"Me, too," Tim said. "Look, my dad put up a basketball hoop in our driveway. Want to come over and shoot baskets with Zach and me?"

Emerson stared at his bike handles. He didn't really like playing basketball. He was much better at soccer. Right now all he wanted to do was kick a soccer ball again and again as hard as he could. But he didn't want to go home, either. He shrugged, "Okay."

He walked his bike alongside his friends to Tim's house. Tim went inside and came out with a new basketball. For a long time, they took turns shooting baskets, but Emerson couldn't concentrate. *I only told them Dad's leaving. I didn't tell them I might be going, too. Later. I'll tell them later.*

They took turns until the sun hovered above the trees. Suddenly, *Star Wars* music jangled in Emerson's pocket. "Oh, geez. I still have Mom's cell." He grunted while fishing it out and pressing the green button. "Yeah?"

Mom's voice sounded bright and cheery, like nothing was wrong. "I just put a pizza in the oven. Be home in twenty minutes."

Emerson grunted again, "Okay." He punched the off button and shoved the phone back in his pocket.

"Dinner call?" Zach palmed the ball.

Emerson nodded.

"I better get home, too." Zach tossed the ball to Tim. "Tomorrow let's all meet at the pool when it opens. We'll figure out what to do after that."

Emerson swung his leg over the bike seat. "Don't know if I can." He took a deep breath and looked over his shoulder at his friends. "I might have to go away this summer." He pushed off and pedaled furiously down the street. He did not look back.

3

My Last Day With Dad

Emerson bolted upright in bed, sweat dripping from his body. He opened his eyes to the blinding sun in his room. It was just a dream. He shook his head, but he couldn't shake the image of his dad being blown up by fierce and evil men wearing strange clothes.

"Emerson," his mother knocked on the bedroom door. "Time to get up. We have lots to do today."

He groaned. *Dad leaves tomorrow. Maybe he has lots to do today, but not me.* Emerson crawled out of bed and headed for the bathroom. *I wish I could stop Dad from leaving, but I can't. Then there's the other problem. Grandpa. I have to get out of that.*

Emerson closed the bathroom door. *I know! If I'm gone, too, Mom will be all alone. I'll tell her all the things I'll do if I stay, like making coffee when she gets*

13

up. By the time he left the bathroom, Emerson thought of other reasons. *I already said I'd help her with homework. I'll take out the trash and load dishes in the dishwasher every day. We can watch Netflix movies and eat popcorn when she's not studying.*

Emerson's brain kept working on reasons why he should stay home. While fishing his jeans out of a drawer, the ace of all ideas flashed through his mind. *What if I go to Grandpa's and something bad happens to me? What if I DIE? Yes! That's it! When I tell her that, she'll be too scared to send me away.*

Pleased with his plan, Emerson dressed quickly and joined Mom and Dad at the kitchen table. *I'll spring it on Mom right after Dad leaves.* Mom was flipping pancakes while Dad set butter and maple syrup on the table.

"Son, what do you want to do today?" Dad sipped his coffee. "It's my last day, and all I have to do is pack."

The question stumped him. "Do? I don't know. It's already hard for me to think you're going away."

"Well, there's an Isotopes baseball game this evening. Why don't the three of us go?"

Emerson felt a lump forming in his throat and he squeezed his eyes shut. When he opened them, a plate of pancakes sat in front of him. He grabbed the syrup and poured a lake over them.

"Dad, what if you get blown up? Last night I dreamed that happened. Then I'd never see you again. You can't go away, you just can't." His voice began

14

shaking, so he shoved a forkful of pancakes in his mouth.

"Emerson, I won't get blown up. My job will keep me in a compound most of the time, not out fighting the enemy."

"Yeah, but Dad, you hear about those crazies ramming trucks into compounds. Everything explodes and people get killed." He jabbed his pancakes for another bite.

Dad reached across the table for Emerson's hand. "Son, I love you and I love your mom. You have to believe that I'll come back safe and sound."

Emerson looked up. "Don't send me away. Let me stay here and have fun with my friends."

His dad straightened up and shook his head. "No, Son. We told you yesterday you're going to your grandfather's."

"But I'll already be missing you, Dad! Now I'll be missing Mom and my friends and all my plans." He grabbed his plate and fork and pushed away from the table.

"Honey, stay and eat breakfast with us," Mom said. "We won't have time tomorrow morning. We have to leave for the airport before five — "

"No!" Emerson jumped up and walked back to his room. Once inside, he slammed the door and turned on TV. He stared at an old Western movie while he ate. He had just finished when he heard a knock on his door.

Go away, he thought. But finally he said, "Okay. Come in."

Mom walked in and sat on the edge of his bed. "Emerson, we're going to spend today together as a family. You can make this a happy memory for your father, or you can make it miserable. Honey, he doesn't want to go away any more than you do. But he has to. Someday you'll understand."

"No, I won't. I'll never understand." He bit his lip.

"Put your shoes on and brush your teeth. This morning we'll ride the tram up to the Crest because that's what your father wants to do. Then we'll come home and pack, and this evening we'll go to the Isotopes game." She smiled and pushed Emerson's hair off his forehead. "That means ball park hot dogs and Coke for dinner."

That was his favorite meal, and usually it made him smile, but not today. Finally he said, "Okay. I better call Zach and tell him." Emerson followed his mom to the kitchen. She started washing dishes while he dialed Zach's home number. He ducked around the corner into the hall and stretched the cord as far as it would go.

"Captain Koury's residence," Zach answered.

Emerson tried to keep his voice low so Mom and Dad wouldn't hear. "Dad's leaving tomorrow so we're spending today together. I can't meet you."

"Man, that's bad. But I hear you. How about tomorrow after your dad leaves?"

"Maybe. Mom has this crazy idea about sending me to my grandfather for the summer. I'll get back with you later."

16

Emerson said good-bye and hung up the phone. Mom had finished the dishes and was putting things inside her purse. Dad stood at the door, tossing his car keys in the air. Emerson's shoulders slumped. *Time to begin our last day.*

4

No Way Out

The buzzing of the alarm startled Emerson awake, and he reached for his glasses. Four o'clock. He groaned and punched the off button. In the next room he heard his parents getting up. His dad walked to the bathroom while his mom went to the kitchen to make coffee. He knew their routine.

Emerson crawled out of bed, dressed quickly and joined Mom in the kitchen. She poured him a bowl of Post Toasties and set milk and sugar on the table. He trickled a tiny bit of milk over his cereal followed by several spoons of sugar.

Dad came to the table, yawning, dressed in his green and tan fatigues. Mom gave him a bowl of cereal and a mug of coffee, then left to get dressed.

"Dad? Will you call us when you get there?"

"Yes, I'll call, but it'll be tomorrow morning before

I land in Afghanistan."

"Can I call you when I want to, or email you?"

"No, Son, you can't. I'll be working in a compound, but it's still a war zone. It'll be better if I email your mom."

Emerson remained silent for a while, watching his father eat. *Dad's so brave, going to war where he might get killed. I'll never be as brave as him. Please, God, don't let him get blown up.*

Mom walked into the kitchen. "Time to go," she said in a strange, tiny voice. Dad picked up his suitcases while Mom opened the front door. The early morning air felt faintly chilly, and Emerson shivered. The sky was dark; the moon had already disappeared below the horizon.

Dad drove silently to the Albuquerque airport. Emerson sat in the back seat, staring out the window. Mom sat in the front seat, sniffling and blowing her nose. In no time they pulled up to the curb for departing flights.

Dad and Mom got out, but Emerson couldn't move. *I can't say good-bye. It's just not fair*! He felt that lump growing in his throat again and was afraid he might cry.

Mom opened his car door. "Please, honey. Come say good-bye."

Emerson slid out and stood next to Dad. An attendant picked up the suitcases and checked his dad's flight ticket.

"Come here, Son," Dad bent over and hugged him hard. "I love you and I'll miss you." Emerson felt something wet dribble down his face and realized his father was crying. *It must hurt Dad to say good-bye, just like it hurts me.* Then his face scrunched up and tears slid from his eyes, too. *My dad's the bravest man in the world. If he can cry, I can, too.*

Dad let him go and hugged Mom. He whispered something to her that Emerson couldn't hear, but it just made Mom cry harder. Then Dad pulled away and backed up, waving to them.

Mom leaned over and pulled Emerson to her side, holding him tight. He wanted to say good-bye, but couldn't choke out any words. Then Dad turned and stepped through the sliding glass door. In moments, he was gone.

The short drive home was quiet, except for crying and sniffing tears up their noses. When Mom unlocked the front door she said, "It's only 5:30. Maybe we should both try to go back to sleep."

Emerson nodded and went to his room. He flopped down on the bed, still dressed in his clothes. When he woke, the sun shone through the window, and his head ached. He sniffed the air. *Brownies! I smell brownies!* He rolled out of bed and headed to the kitchen. Mom sat at the table reading the morning paper. A plate of brownies sat next to her coffee mug.

Emerson slid into his chair and bit into one.

"Brownies, Mom? We never get to eat them this early."

She set the paper down and smiled, "I felt hungry for them." She took a deep breath. "Now that Dad's gone, we need to talk about sending you to Grandpa's for the summer."

"Mom, I can't go. What if something happens to Dad, and I'm not here?" He leaned forward and stared into her eyes. He had to make her change her mind. "What if something happens to ME?" He lowered his voice. "What if I DIE or something and you're not with me?"

Mom shook her head. "Nothing will happen to you — "

The kitchen phone rang, interrupting her. She lifted the receiver. "Captain Wright's residence." She nodded slightly and glanced at Emerson. "Hello, Dad. Yes, Ben left this morning."

Emerson pushed his chair back from the table. *It's Grandpa.* He watched his mother closely while she talked.

"Yes, that's still the plan," Mom said. "But he's not exactly…thrilled…about spending the summer with you."

"Not exactly thrilled?" Emerson jumped up. "Mom, I'm so mad I could hit something! I don't want to go!"

Mom frowned and shook her head in warning. "Yes, Dad, that was Emerson. Leaving home for the summer is a shock, especially with his father deployed. But he'll get used to being with you."

Emerson shook his head back and forth and dragged his finger across his throat. "I'm not going, Mom."

She held up her hand like a traffic cop and mouthed "Stop."

"Here's the bus information, Dad. It leaves Albuquerque at nine o'clock tomorrow morning, scheduled to arrive in Gallup at a quarter to one. I'm sending your picture with him so he'll know who you are."

Emerson jumped up and slammed his chair against the table. "Tomorrow? You're making me go *tomorrow?*"

For a minute Mom looked like she might cry again. "Dad, I have to go. Please, just be there to get him." She was quiet for a moment. Then she whispered, "Thank you," and hung up.

Just like that? I'm doomed! Emerson ran to his room and slammed the door. He threw himself on his bed and punched the pillow. His stomach felt tied up in knots, and his mind frantically searched for a way out.

There was a knock on his door. "Emerson, it's Mom."

Duh! Who else would it be?

"I'm coming in." The door opened and Mom walked through. She sat on the bed next to him. "Honey, I know this isn't what you want. But I want you to get to know your grandpa. He has a different way of life and a different culture to teach you."

"If that's so great, why don't you teach me? Then I could stay here."

Mom was quiet for so long, Emerson thought she forgot his question. Finally, she said, "Emerson, I can't take care of you this summer. Your grandpa can. Why don't you get up now and go hang out with your friends? After dinner, we'll pack your suitcase. We're not talking about this anymore." She stood and walked out.

Emerson closed his eyes and images of sheep and a faceless stranger floated in his mind. *No! I won't think about him.* He rolled off the bed and walked to the kitchen to call Zach.

That night after dinner, Mom placed an empty suitcase on Emerson's bed.

"I won't pack anything," Emerson said, crossing his arms over his chest. "If you're in such a hurry to get rid of me, you do it."

He heard his Mom suck in her breath, but she didn't say anything. Instead, she opened his dresser drawers and pulled out underwear, socks, shirts, and jeans. Then she walked to the bathroom and returned with new packages of toothpaste, a toothbrush, hairbrush and several bars of soap. Finally she pulled down a box from the closet shelf and opened it. Inside was a pair of brand new cowboy boots. She placed them in the suitcase on top of the clothes.

She's only packing clothes? What about my stuff? Emerson reached for his laptop and put it in the suitcase. He turned around for his iPod when Mom said, "No, honey, you can't take those." She picked up the laptop.

"Can't take them?" He turned back to his Mom. "Why not?"

"Emerson, you're going to sheep camp. That's out on the mesa. There's no WiFi out there, and no place to plug in a battery charger."

"WHAT?" Emerson grabbed the laptop from her hands. "That's not fair! You can't make me go someplace where I can't have fun."

"I'm sorry, but that's the way it is. You can pack some books."

"I hate this! And I hate you! Dad wouldn't make me go away!" Emerson clutched his laptop to his chest and stormed out of the room.

His mother called after him, "Honey, this was his idea."

Emerson stopped in his tracks. *Dad betrayed me, too?* He felt like someone just punched him in the stomach.

5

I'm Doomed

Emerson slumped in his seat and kicked the empty one in front of him. *Just great, stuck on a bus going nowhere. What's even worse, when I get there, I have to herd sheep! My whole summer – wasted on stupid sheep!*

He drained the last of his bottled water. *Mom made me get on this bus. But she can't make me like living with Grandpa. She can't make me like herding sheep. And she can't keep me from running away when I get the chance.*

He'd tossed and turned last night and didn't get much sleep. He wolfed down the sandwich Mom packed for him when the bus stopped in Grants. But he was still tired, hungry and thirsty.

At last the bus slowed down, and Emerson looked out the window. Gallup, New Mexico, the sign read.

Wherever that is! He groaned and kicked the front seat again. The bus carried him closer and closer to meeting his grandfather, closer and closer to wasting his entire summer on the Navajo reservation.

The bus turned into the station and stopped. Passengers crowded the aisle, rushing to get off.

"Okay Emerson, it's time to go." The bus driver smiled and held out his hand. "Come on, now."

Emerson glared at the driver. "I can get up myself. I don't need your help." He stood and pushed past the outstretched hand, stomping through the aisle and down the steps. Outside the bus, Emerson stopped and took a photo from his shirt pocket. It showed a strange old man staring straight at the camera. He wore a high crown, flat brimmed black hat, and he didn't smile. *Great, just great. A grump for a grandfather.*

Emerson pushed the bridge of his glasses firmly against his face while people pushed past him. He looked around and saw a lot of men wearing the same black hat. He took a few steps forward and looked again at the photo. The bus driver walked right behind him. *He's supposed to make sure I find Grandpa. Mom thinks I'm still a baby.*

"Do you see your grandfather?" the bus driver asked.

Emerson shook his head. *And I'm not looking for him anymore, either. I'll tell Mom he didn't show up.* Quickly he turned and headed back to the bus.

"Emerson!" A deep voice jolted him to a stop. "Come back. Your grandfather is right here."

Slowly he turned and squinted up at the stranger walking toward him. Then he looked down at the photo in his hand. "You don't look like him."

The stranger dropped to one knee. "I'm Charlie Nakai, father to your mother and grandfather to you." He held out a photo. "Your mother sent this to me."

Emerson stared at it. The picture was taken a few months ago at one of his soccer games. He was sitting with Mom and Dad, and they were all laughing about something. He wished he could remember what was so funny.

Emerson pushed his glasses with his finger and looked up. "Okay. So, maybe you are my grandpa. But Mom made a big mistake. I'm going home." He turned toward the bus.

Grandpa Charlie grabbed his arm. "No, Emerson. Your mother wants you to spend the summer here." He stood and looked toward the bus. "Which suitcase is yours?"

"This is it." The bus driver retrieved it from the luggage bin and handed it to Grandpa Charlie. "Have fun with your grandpa, Emerson."

Emerson grunted and crossed his arms over his chest. *Yeah. Right. Like that'll ever happen.*

"Thank you," Grandpa Charlie nodded to the driver. "Come, Emerson."

29

Emerson stood rooted in place, feeling doomed. There was no turning around now, no going back.

Grandpa Charlie gripped Emerson's shoulder and pushed him forward. They walked toward a dusty brown pickup truck holding two large tanks strapped down in the bed.

Emerson stared at them for a moment. *What are those for? Nope. Not gonna ask.*

Throwing the suitcase between the tanks, Grandpa Charlie told him to get in. As soon as they settled on the seat, he said, "First, we will call your mother." His grandfather pulled a cell phone from the glove compartment and a scrap of yellow paper from his pocket. Slowly, he punched in some numbers.

Emerson squirmed. *It's taking too long. I bet he got voice mail. I bet Mom's not even home.* He gestured to his grandfather to give him the phone.

Grandpa Charlie finally spoke. "Tina, Emerson is with me. He wants to talk to you." Emerson grabbed the phone.

"Mom?" Silence. *Voice mail. I was right.* His stomach knotted up. "Mom, don't make me stay here. I want to come…" A beeping sound interrupted him, followed by silence. His throat tightened. *Mom's not even home waiting for my call. I bet she's happy she got rid of me.* He shoved the phone back at his grandfather.

Grandpa Charlie started the truck, and before long, they drove north out of Gallup.

Emerson stared at the strange-looking countryside. *It's so different from Albuquerque. The mountains are a lot shorter and reddish and weird, like Mars.*

Grandpa Charlie cleared his throat. "Your mother tells me you play soccer."

I'm not talking to him. Emerson stared out his window.

The old man waited for an answer. After a minute, he tried again. "I understand you do homework on a computer."

Keep talking. It won't get you anywhere. Emerson continued staring out the window.

Several minutes passed before Grandpa Charlie spoke again. "Did you see the tanks in back? They're empty now. We'll pick up fresh water before driving to camp."

So that's what they're for. But why pick up fresh water? Doesn't Grandpa have faucets?

A while passed before his grandfather spoke again. "Did you know the Navajo word for sheep is **dibe**? Can you say that?"

Of course I can. But you can't make me. Silence hung between them like a damp curtain.

Grandpa Charlie sighed. "**Shi Tsoi**, have you forgotten your voice? Maybe you left it home with your mother."

Emerson jerked his head around, glaring at the old man.

31

"It doesn't matter." Grandpa Charlie followed the curve of the road. "Our *dibe* will not care if you don't talk."

Days of pent up anger suddenly exploded. "You don't understand!" Emerson uttered through clenched teeth. "I don't want to be here! I don't want to herd sheep! I don't want to be a Navajo!" He glared at his grandfather. "And I don't want to waste my summer with you!"

Grandpa Charlie pulled over and stopped on the shoulder of the road. His voice was firm. "I know you don't want to be here, but you cannot go home. You are *Shi Tsoi*, my grandson. I want to teach you about being *Diné. Diné* means Navajo."

Emerson wiped his glasses with his sleeve and looked at his grandfather. Grandpa Charlie had an old face, full of wrinkles. He wore his hair in a bun behind his neck like an old lady, and he smelled like tobacco and sagebrush. His dark eyes reminded Emerson of his mother's eyes. But it wasn't enough. This old man wasn't his family. And the Navajo reservation wasn't his home.

Emerson turned his face to the window again. "You're just a stranger." Resentment crept back into his voice. "I don't belong here. I'll never be happy."

Grandpa Charlie started the truck. "We'll stop in Bobcat Ridge for water and supplies before driving to camp."

It was early afternoon, but Emerson felt worn out

from the bus ride. He leaned his head against the window and stared at the scenery rushing by. His thoughts returned to his home and his friends going to the pool and the racetrack without him.

I'm all by myself. Dad's gone, and Mom doesn't love me anymore. It hurt to think about that, so he tried not to think. Instead, he played "pretend" in his mind. Pretending his dad never left for Afghanistan, and he was home with his friends having the best summer of his life.

Time passed in this daydream until his grandfather slowed down. The truck turned into a parking lot and rolled to a stop in front of a building. Emerson looked up at the sign over the door: Bobcat Ridge Trading Post.

Grandpa Charlie turned off the ignition and honked the horn.

The sudden sound startled Emerson, and he reached for his door handle. His grandfather leaned over and stopped him. "No," he said. "It's polite to wait."

6

Nothing Makes Sense

"Huh?" Grandpa's words baffled Emerson.

"**Shi Tsoi.** When we park at the trading post, we honk and wait a moment before getting out. When we arrive at a **hogan**, where people live, we honk and then wait in the truck until they invite us in."

He hated to ask, but curiosity nagged at him. "Why?"

"To let the people we are visiting know we are here so they can be ready. It is the Navajo way."

Emerson wrinkled his nose. "Every time?"

Grandpa Charlie nodded. "Especially when we park in front of a **hogan**. When we are polite, we show respect." He opened his door. "It's been long enough."

That's just weird. Emerson slid out and closed his door. *This is a trading post? It looks more like a store. Not like those in western movies.* He followed his grandfather up a few steps and through a screen door.

"*Ya'at'eeh*, Charlie." A woman's voice greeted them. Emerson turned and saw a short round woman with a big grin standing behind the counter. "Here for supplies?"

"*Ya'at'eeh*, Jolene. Yes, pack the usual...flour, beans, cornmeal, jerky, canned vegetables and fruit, coffee, lard, sugar..." He tipped his head toward Emerson. "And a sack of hard candy."

Jolene grinned and waved to Emerson. "So you're Charlie's grandson. Welcome to the Rez."

Emerson looked down at his feet. This lady seemed nice and friendly, but he didn't feel like smiling back. Instead, he said, "Do you have any comic books? Or any books at all?"

"Right over there." She motioned with her chin to a rack at the end of the wall. Emerson walked over and pulled out a Spiderman comic.

Jolene lowered her voice. "How's it going with the boy?"

Emerson glanced at the adults. He heard what she said. *I bet they'll talk about me.* He edged slowly closer to the counter, his face buried in his comic book.

Grandpa Charlie laid his flat brimmed black hat on the counter. Then he clasped his hands and leaned forward on his arms.

"Not well." He kept his voice low. "*Shi Tsoi* is angry

and resents being here. He barely speaks to me."

Emerson took a step closer, still looking at Spiderman.

Jolene shook her head. "You told me his father was deployed and his mother started nursing school. Doesn't he understand?"

"No, he doesn't. I think he feels his parents betrayed him. And this is summer, a time for boys to have fun with their friends. I am nothing to him but a strange old man."

"Well, I hope things change, for both of you." She reached for a cardboard box. "I'll pack your supplies. Drive around back. Joe will help you fill the water tanks. I'll leave your supplies outside the back door. They'll be easier to load while the tanks fill."

Grandpa Charlie paused to look at his grandson before walking out the door, but Emerson turned away. When the truck started, Emerson walked to the screen door. He watched his grandfather drive around the side of the building. Letting out a long breath, he leaned his forehead against the wall.

I don't know what to think anymore. I feel like that dead butterfly pinned to the board in class.

Rustling sounds interrupted his thoughts and he looked around. Jolene walked up to him carrying a small sack in one hand and a big tube in the other.

"Here's some candy. Your grandfather wanted you to have it." She handed him the sack.

Emerson nodded shyly and thanked her. Then he stuffed the bag inside his jeans pocket.

"And here's the biggest tube of sunscreen I have." She handed it to him. "It's 45 proof. Your skin is pretty pale, more like your father's. You'll burn and blister in this sun."

"I never wear sunscreen, and I always get a better tan than my friends," he said.

Jolene smiled. "Maybe so. But you'll be in the sun from sun-up to sundown, and you're whiter than most people on the Rez." She pushed a strand of hair off his forehead. "But you have your mother's hair, thick and black."

At the mention of his mother, Emerson bit his lip. "I want to go home. But nobody cares what I want."

Jolene shook her head. "It's different out here, I know. But give it some time. You'll get used to it. And you'll get used to your grandfather."

The sound of a truck's engine startled Emerson, and he looked out the screen door. Grandpa Charlie rolled to a stop in front of the steps and beckoned Emerson with his hand.

"I guess that means I have to go," he grumbled. He held the comic book out to Jolene.

She shook her head. "You keep it." Then she opened the door and scooted him out. "Come back and see me when you're ready for more candy." She gave him a quick hug. "Believe me, you'll get used to life out here."

No, I won't. Emerson stomped down the steps and yanked the passenger door open. Sliding in, he slammed the door shut and folded his arms across his chest.

Grandpa Charlie eased the truck out onto the highway and headed toward sheep camp. It was a long time before either one spoke.

7
A Bad Start

 Emerson squinted at the sun in the western sky and checked his watch. *Only 4:30? I've been traveling all day, and we're not even there yet.*

Grandpa Charlie turned off the highway and drove slowly down a bumpy dirt road.

What an awful place! We're in the middle of nowhere. And it's so dusty. He rolled up his window to shut out the dust. *Yuck! I can still taste it!*

He felt a sinking feeling in his stomach. *What's Mom doing? Does she miss me yet? What're the guys doing right now?* Emerson clenched his teeth. *I hate this place already.*

His grandfather turned onto a path barely wide enough for the truck. It felt like forever before they finally drove over a small hill and rolled to a stop.

To the right, Emerson saw several large brush and pole corrals, one tethered horse and a horse trailer. Over to the left he noticed a bunch of footlockers and a fire pit covered with a grill. Beyond that, a small structure with a roof caught his eye. It was open on one side.

"Is this sheep camp?" Emerson asked.

His grandfather nodded.

"Where are all the buildings? I watched a movie about a sheep ranch in Australia. They had lots of buildings."

"We have no buildings out here. This is a summer camp, not a ranch."

"Oh." *Sure not what I expected.* Emerson looked around. "So where are all the sheep? I don't see any." A peculiar smell hung in the air, and he wrinkled his nose.

Grandpa Charlie jutted his chin toward a small hill. "Here they come now. The **dibe**, our sheep. The man on horseback is my friend Sam. Look over there. Do you see that black dog? We have another one at the back of the herd. Our sheepdogs."

"So they keep the sheep together in a pack?" Emerson watched the black dog circling the front of the herd. He remembered seeing sheepdogs in the movie, but they looked different. More hair, he thought.

"Yes. We could not herd this many without them."

"Oh." *I guess I should act interested.* "Do you own lots of sheep?" Emerson tried counting, but there were too many of them.

"We have ninety-eight *dibe* and seventeen *ti'izi*. *Ti'izi* are goats. But I do not own them. In *Diné*, the women own the family herds. Many sheepherders are women."

The boy turned to his grandfather. "If you don't own them, Grandpa, who does?"

"My wife, your grandmother, owned them in life. She had no sisters, only brothers. Men don't inherit the family herd. When her spirit passed, my daughter, your mother, became the owner."

"What?" Emerson's mouth fell open. "You mean Mom owns them?" He wrinkled his nose again.

"Yes. I tend them for her. Sam is an old friend and helps when I must be away from camp. Like today, when I drove to Gallup."

Emerson shook his head. "Why would Mom want a bunch of old sheep? She should sell them."

The old man sucked his breath between his teeth and stared straight ahead.

An uneasy feeling gripped Emerson's stomach. *Uh-oh. I said something wrong. I wish I'd never started talking to him.* He turned and looked out the side window. *I just don't belong here. I'll never get used to it. Never!*

Grandpa Charlie opened his door. "Enough talk." He jutted his chin toward three corrals. "Those are *bighans* where the *dibe* sleep each night. You can watch from here. Do not leave the truck."

Grandpa Charlie stepped out and grabbed a rope

44

from the bed of the truck. Waving it in front of him, he began driving *dibe* into the middle *dibe bighan*.

"Stay here, he says," Emerson grumbled. "He just thinks I'll get in the way." He opened the door. "Well, Mom and Dad aren't here, and I don't have to do what he says."

Emerson scooted out of the truck. The scene before him bustled with activity, and the smell of sheep hung in the air. The *dibe* crowded toward their *bighans*, kicking up large clouds of dust. He walked closer.

Suddenly something rammed his butt and sent him sprawling in the dirt. Scrambling to his feet, Emerson quickly spun around. Staring at him a few feet away was the biggest goat he'd ever seen. It had a wild look in its eyes.

Emerson swung his fist at the goat. "Bad goat. Go away!"

The goat lowered its head and charged.

He tried jumping out of the way but the goat butted him in the stomach. "Ooomph!" Emerson landed on his butt, the breath knocked out of him. The goat stood still, staring at him.

"Back off, you stupid goat!" He took a few deep breaths. Then leaning to one side, he pushed himself to his knees. The goat lowered its head and pawed the ground. It stood between him and the truck.

Oh no! It's coming for me again! Emerson scrambled to his feet and stumbled toward the sheep herd.

They scattered in front of the goat, leaving Emerson no protection.

"Help! Grandpa, help!" The words were out of his mouth before he could stop them. He grabbed a sheep trying to use it as a shield, but the goat charged around it. Emerson let go and ran inside the closest *dibe bighan*. The goat butted him again, and he hit the dirt with a thud.

Emerson raised his head, feeling dizzy, his throat choked with dust. The goat stood a few feet away, watching.

Where's Grandpa? Didn't he hear me? Slowly he looked up and over his shoulder. The sheep walked to one side and now he saw his grandfather and Sam. They stood right inside the *dibe bighan* next to the open gate. Emerson's eyes narrowed. They were looking at him and laughing.

What? That goat knocked me down and they're LAUGHING?

Angry now, Emerson jumped to his feet and raced toward his grandfather, the goat hot on his heels. Grandpa Charlie rushed past him waving the rope and yelling at the goat in Navajo. Emerson sprinted through the gate and toward the truck. He yanked the door open, jumped inside and slammed it shut.

He sat there alone, panting and watching his grandfather and Sam. The two men and sheepdogs herded the rest of the sheep and goats into all three *dibe bighans*.

Emerson's resentment grew while he watched. *I'm tired. I'm thirsty. I'm hungry. That goat butted me and Grandpa just laughed. I gotta get out of here.* He looked over his shoulder at the mesa behind him. *Which way do I go? Where's a map?*

He opened the glove compartment and found a small package of peanuts. Ripping it open with his teeth, he poured the peanuts into his mouth and chomped until they were gone. Then he rummaged through the glove compartment. No map. He slumped down in his seat.

Finally Grandpa Charlie returned. He opened Emerson's door and motioned for him to get out.

"The *dibe* are counted and penned," he said. "The dogs are hungry. Feeding them will be your job this summer." He paused for a moment. "You may be angry at Old Jack. He's a mean goat, but a good leader. The other goats and sheep follow him."

Emerson glowered at his grandfather. "So what? You laughed when you saw Old Jack hurting me! My friends' grandpas wouldn't do that. Their grandpas are nice."

The old man lowered his eyes, a slight smile on his lips. "I don't think you are hurt. I think you are just embarrassed. Old Jack goes after everyone. Sometimes even me. Perhaps I shouldn't have laughed, but it was funny. I waved him off before he could butt you again."

Emerson stared at the ground, his face flushed with anger.

"You run pretty fast when you want to."

48

Emerson glared up at his grandfather. "I don't think that's funny." He turned away from the old man and spotted the fire pit. His stomach growled. "I'm hungry, Grandpa." He said. "And I need a drink of water. When can we eat dinner?"

"Soon." Grandpa Charlie beckoned Emerson to follow him. "The dog food is over in that bin. Two bowls are inside. Fill them to the top. While you do that, I'll start dinner." He turned and walked toward the fire pit.

Emerson had to walk past the first *dibe bighan* to reach the food bin. He noticed Old Jack staring at him through the poles. Emerson shook his fist at him. *I'll get even with you before I get out of here. This isn't over. Not by a long shot.*

8

This Isn't for Me

Emerson woke suddenly when a hand shook his shoulder.

"**Shi Tsoi.**" His grandfather squatted beside him. "The sun is rising. Time to wake up."

Emerson sat up and squinted at the pink horizon. Here on the ground it was gray and shadowy, and he was still sleepy.

"Get dressed and come eat breakfast." Grandpa Charlie stood and jutted his chin at the campfire. "We have a long day ahead of us."

Emerson rubbed his eyes and crawled out of the sleeping bag. He sniffed the air and his mouth began to water. Quickly he yanked on his jeans and pulled his T-shirt over his head. He'd slept with his socks on, so he pushed his feet into his boots. Then he joined his grandfather.

Emerson looked around. "Where's Sam?"

"He left early this morning while you slept. Here." Grandpa Charlie handed him a tin plate with beans, fry bread, and a slice of ham. It was the weirdest breakfast he'd ever seen. He scooped some beans on the fry bread and took a bite. *Hey, this is really good. Zach will probably eat boring old cereal when he gets up.*

His grandfather handed him a cup filled with a fruity smelling liquid. He took a sip. *Tastes okay, maybe it's Kool-Aid.* He looked around while he ate, thinking this place looked familiar. *I know! Like a cattle drive in those TV movies. Something exciting always happens, like stampedes and fighting cattle rustlers.*

He was sipping whatever it was when memories of pancakes with Mom and Dad flashed through his mind. A lump rose in his throat, and he set his plate on the ground.

"Grandpa?" He felt uncomfortable talking to him, but he waited for his grandfather to look at him. "What'll we do next? After breakfast?"

His grandfather poured the last of the coffee from the pot. "First, we herd the *dibe* to the grazing grounds. We watch them so they stay together and don't stray off. If they eat most of the grass, we'll move them to another place. When the sun is about there," he pointed to a place in the sky, "we will bring them back to camp."

Emerson's mouth dropped open. *That's it? He can't mean me, too. I'd waste my whole day.* He spoke slowly. "Well, Grandpa, what'll I do while you're watching the sheep?"

"**Shi Tsoi**, you will watch the **dibe** with me."

Dismay flooded Emerson's face. *What? Man, I'm gonna hate this. I should have brought my iPod and my comic books.*

"Your face tells me you are not pleased," Grandpa Charlie said. "Sheep mean life to the Navajo people. You will learn much this summer."

Emerson kicked a dirt clod into the fire. "Mom wouldn't make me do this. She'd find something fun for me to do."

The old man's face grew stern. "Your mother is not here." He tossed the remainder of his coffee on the campfire and wiped out the pot. "Finish eating and clean your plate and fork. Rub them with sand then wipe them off. Put them inside the footlocker and meet me at the first **bighan**." He stood and walked away.

Emerson glared at the old man's back and chugged the last of his drink. Scraping his plate and fork with sand, he muttered under his breath, "If he thinks I'm spending every day staring at sheep, he's crazy! First chance I get, I'm outta here."

Grandpa Charlie called his name, and Emerson groaned. He shoved his plate and fork inside a footlocker and shuffled slowly toward the old man. *Why me? Could this get any worse?*

Grandpa Charlie hooked a canteen onto Emerson's belt. Then he helped Emerson with the straps of a small backpack. "Now you have water and food for the day. It's a long walk to the grazing ground."

"What?" Emerson pointed to two horses tethered nearby. "Can't we ride them?"

"*Shi Tsoi*, some days we ride. But today we walk. It's the best way for you to learn."

"Oh, geez," Emerson grumbled. *It just got worse.*

Grandpa Charlie ignored the comment and handed his grandson a walking stick. Then he opened the first *dibe bighan*, and sheep poured out of the corral. Emerson dodged around and between them until he stood next to his grandfather.

"Walk with the *dibe*." His grandfather pointed. "See where Red herds them?" Emerson shaded his glasses and spotted the older dog. Red herded them in one direction by crouching and springing until they all moved together.

Grandpa Charlie nudged Emerson's shoulder. "See the black dog, Flint? He will bring up the rear and keep them moving in the same direction."

Breathing a loud sigh, Emerson trailed behind his grandfather. He turned once to watch the sheep behind him and spotted Old Jack. *No! Not him.* Quickly he caught up with Grandpa Charlie and looked behind him again. *That stupid old goat didn't see me. He's way over on the other side.* But just to be safe, Emerson circled to the other side of his grandfather. *I'll keep Grandpa between me and Old Jack.*

They walked and walked and walked. The sun rose

in the sky and began beating down on Emerson's bare head. Too late he remembered the sunscreen Jolene had given him. His neck already felt hot and sore. *Ugh. My tongue's stuck to the roof of my mouth. I need water.*

Emerson stopped, unhooked his canteen and took a swig.

His grandfather reached for the canteen. "Do not gulp. Let the water roll around in your mouth. Then swallow."

He unzipped Emerson's backpack and pulled out a floppy hat and bandana. "Here, tie this around your neck." He plopped the hat on Emerson's head. It was way too big and the crown touched Emerson's eyebrows. "It will keep the sun off your face for now. We'll buy a better hat next time we go to Bobcat Ridge."

Emerson rolled his eyes. *Bet I look stupid. At least I don't have to squint so much.* He took another sip from his canteen and plodded on beside Grandpa Charlie. Now and then he looked around to make sure Old Jack didn't sneak up on him.

Finally they reached a spot where the *dibe* could graze. Emerson crawled under the shade of a big bush. His stomach rumbled, so he pulled an apple from his backpack. At least Grandpa knew to pack food. While he ate, his thoughts returned to his friends at home, having fun without him. *And here I am, stuck out here with nothing to do. It's not fair. I didn't leave Dad and Mom. They left me.*

Just as he feared, the day slowly dragged on. Sometimes the herd shifted and Emerson followed the sheepdogs, watching how they worked. But mostly he was bored stiff. Just when he thought he couldn't stand it anymore, Grandpa Charlie whistled to the dogs.

Red and Flint rounded up the stragglers and turned the *dibe* back in the direction they'd traveled. Suddenly Old Jack trotted right in front of his eyes toward the front of the herd.

Emerson froze in his tracks. *I'm gonna stay behind him so he won't see me.*

Old Jack suddenly broke away from the herd and turned around. Their eyes met, and they stared hard at each other. Jack took a step forward. Emerson held his breath. Jack lowered his head and pawed the ground. Then Grandpa Charlie waved his arms and yelled at the goat. Jack backed away and returned to his post in front of the sheep.

Emerson heaved a big sigh of relief. *Old Jack still wants to bully me. How can I make him stop?* He pounded his fist into his other hand. *He's just a goat. I'm a boy, and boys are smarter than goats. I have to think of something.*

He thought and thought all the way back to camp. He concentrated so hard that Grandpa Charlie had to tell him several times to get out of the way and close the gates. By dinnertime, he gave up. *I may be smarter, but Jack's bigger and faster than me. And he's meaner. I gotta stay out of his way. If Grandpa would let me ride a horse, then Jack couldn't bother me.*

Holding the burrito his grandfather cooked, Emerson plopped down at the campfire. Images of his long, boring day floated through his mind, followed by day after boring day for the rest of the summer. *No way I'm staying here.* He chomped on his burrito. *If Indians can find the way out of this mesa, then so can I.*

9
I Hate It Here

 I've been here a whole week. Emerson groaned, plodding along with the **dibe**. He looked around at the mesa and the distant mountains. *At home there's always something fun to do. Out here there's nothing but work.*

Every now and then Emerson scanned the sheep herd for Old Jack. He didn't want the goat surprising him. "Cripes," he muttered. "I'm sick and tired of that old goat. I'm sick and tired of herding sheep. I miss my computer. I miss playing soccer with my friends. I miss Mom. I miss Dad. If he hadn't gone to Afghanistan, I'd be home right now." He stopped talking to himself. It just made him feel worse.

That night after dinner, Emerson sat on the log next to his grandfather. Talking to Grandpa Charlie made Emerson really nervous. He cleared his throat and fidgeted, waiting for his grandfather to notice him.

Finally, Grandpa Charlie said, "Do you have something to say?"

Emerson blurted out, "I want to go home. Can we go to town and call Mom?"

Grandpa Charlie stared into the campfire for a minute. At last he said, "**Shi Tsoi**, you cannot go home, not until school starts. You know that already."

"Awww, Grandpa…"

Grandpa Charlie held up his hand. "However, we can try to call your mother."

"Really? When? Your phone won't work out here."

"We are going to the Chapter House tomorrow night. There's a cell phone tower nearby. We can call her there."

Emerson grinned. *Okay, at least I got one thing I wanted. I'll bet Mom is so lonely by now, she lets me come home.* He stood up. "Okay Grandpa. I'm going to play with Red and Flint now." Emerson ran over to pet the dogs.

The following afternoon, they brought the **dibe** back to camp early. His grandfather filled a bucket with water so Emerson could wash the sweat and dirt off. While Emerson put on a clean shirt and jeans, Grandpa Charlie washed up and changed.

They fed the dogs, jumped in the truck, and were on their way to the Chapter House. Emerson daydreamed about hanging out with Zach and Tim again. But he'd miss playing with Red and Flint. *I wish I had a dog of my own. I'll ask Mom for one when I get home.*

Grandpa Charlie's voice brought him out of his daydream. "***Shi Tsoi***, do you know what the Chapter House is?"

"Huh? No. I remember Mom and Dad talked about it. But it sounded like grown-up stuff." He shrugged.

His grandfather looked at him for a few seconds before shaking his head. "We go there to elect councilors to represent us in tribal government. We also meet there to discuss things important to our community and the reservation."

Emerson nodded. It sounded so boring. "So, is something happening tonight? Or are we going just to call Mom?"

"Tonight we'll hear speeches from people running for office."

"But we can still call Mom first, right? Maybe she'll want me home right away."

His grandfather frowned. "We will try your mother first. But we're staying for the speeches. I want to hear what they have to say."

Emerson wrinkled his nose. First a boring day with sheep and now a boring night listening to grown-ups stand around and talk.

Finally, Grandpa Charlie slowed down and Emerson saw the Chapter House ahead. The parking area was full of trucks. Looking down at his watch, his grandfather said, "We are late. I may have missed some of the speakers."

"Grandpa, call Mom first before we go in. You said you would."

His grandfather pulled out his phone and punched in the number. Putting the phone to his ear, he said, "It's ringing." Grandpa Charlie lifted his eyebrows and shook his head at Emerson. Then he handed the phone to him. "You can leave a message."

Emerson's throat tightened. The beep sounded, but suddenly, he didn't know what to say. "Hi Mom. It's me. Emerson. Uhmm. I, I… let me come home. I'm really lonely. I don't have any friends here. Uhmm…." The beep sounded again. Emerson stared at the phone and handed it back to his grandfather. His chest hurt, and he couldn't speak.

Grandpa Charlie said nothing but reached across and opened Emerson's door. Slowly, Emerson slid out and closed the door behind him. He followed his grandfather to the Chapter House.

The front door opened and three boys walked out. Grandpa Charlie stopped in front of them.

"*Ya'at'eeh, Hosteen* Nakai," the tallest one said.

"*Ya'at'eeh*, Will." Grandpa Charlie nodded to the others as well. "This is Emerson, my grandson." He nudged Emerson forward. "He's visiting me this summer. Perhaps he can hang out with you."

Grandpa Charlie turned and walked through the

door before Emerson could say anything. Emerson faced the three boys and tried to smile. One appeared to be older than him. The others, he couldn't tell. They stared at him but didn't smile back.

"Hi," Emerson felt shy all of a sudden. No one answered him. "So … what are you guys doing?" He dug his hands into his pockets.

The tall one, Will, said, "You're not really Navajo, are you?"

That surprised Emerson. "Huh? My Mom's Navajo. That's my grandpa in there."

"We already know that," Another boy stepped forward. "I'm John and this here's Frankie. All our parents are Navajo."

Emerson nodded, but he felt awkward. Did he really look that different from them? No one said anything, and that bothered him. "So, do you guys live here?" What a dumb question! He wished he could take it back.

"Yeah," Frankie said. "During the summer. We go away to boarding school the rest of the time. Most kids around here go to boarding school or ride the bus to Shiprock or Newcomb."

"Oh." Emerson shifted his weight. "Well, do you want to know about me?"

"No," John said. "We probably won't see you again after tonight."

Will stepped closer. "If you go to town or see other Navajo boys, be careful. Some of them don't like *bilagaanas*. Your mom might be Navajo, but you're a *bilagaana*."

Emerson flushed deep red and clenched his fists. "I know what that means. Now you're making me mad."

"Hey," Will put up both hands and stepped back. "I'm just telling you to be careful." He looked at his two friends. "We don't care, but some people do. That's all."

The three boys sat on the ground with their backs against the building and started talking. They didn't ask Emerson to join them.

Emerson walked away, looking out into the mesa. The sun hovered low in the sky. Maybe it was almost time to go. *And what about dinner? I'm hungry.*

Then the door opened and someone said, "Better come in. We're already eating."

The three boys jumped up and jostled with each other through the door. Emerson followed behind. He spotted his grandfather talking to another man and walked toward him. Grandpa Charlie held a plate of food. Waving to the food table, he said, "Eat quickly, *Shi Tsoi*. We must leave soon."

Emerson turned to a table filled with dishes of food and grabbed a plate and fork. *Macaroni and cheese!* He shoveled three large servings on his plate. At the end of the table sat one last slice of chocolate cake, an end piece with lots of frosting. He darted around the table and snatched it.

64

Emerson sat across from his grandfather and the other man, eating quickly. Licking chocolate frosting off his fingers, he looked around. The room was full of strangers, strangers with families, all of them laughing and talking. They belonged here. He didn't.

Grandpa Charlie stood up. "*Shi Tsoi,* we must get back to the *dibe.*" He nodded to the other man and said "*Hagoone.*" Emerson already knew this meant good-bye.

He followed his grandfather back to the truck. Once inside, Grandpa Charlie took out his phone. "We can call your mother again. She may be home now."

Emerson stared at the phone and felt a knot in his stomach. He nodded. His grandfather punched in the number again and waited. "No answer. Do you want to leave another message?"

Emerson clenched his jaw and slowly shook his head. "What's the use?" he whispered. "She doesn't care."

Grandpa Charlie started the truck and pulled out onto the road. "I believe your mother does care, *Shi Tsoi,*" he said in a quiet voice. "Someday you may understand."

Emerson turned his head and stared out the window. *No, I won't. No one wants me. Mom doesn't. Grandpa doesn't. I'm only here because Mom made him take me. And those guys back there, they didn't want to be friends.*

He leaned his forehead against the window, feeling more alone than ever.

10

I Really Mess Up

"My worst vacation ever." Emerson plodded along, talking to the *dibe*. He might as well talk to them. No one else listened to him anyway. "I've been stuck here two weeks. I'm so bored I could spit!" He jabbed his walking stick at the ground. "You know why? First Grandpa and me walk and walk and walk to where you graze." He held up his hand. "But wait, there's more. We watch and watch and watch while you *dibe* eat. And that takes you all day." He kicked dirt into little dust clouds. "Then we walk and walk and walk back to camp."

At first he watched for any chance to escape, but his grandfather kept an eye on him. *Even if he didn't, the mesa goes on forever. There's no one out here but us. And he'd just come after me.* When Emerson first heard coyotes howling, his grandfather said they hunt animals at night and eat them. "Sometimes, they even hunt boys and girls," he said. Maybe he imagined it, but Emerson thought he saw his grandfather smile.

No way I'm running away at night!

By the time he finished eating dinner that night, Emerson felt like kicking more than dirt. He sat next to his grandfather. "Grandpa?" Emerson still felt a little nervous talking to him.

Grandpa Charlie nodded.

"I want to do something different tomorrow. I think I know everything about herding sheep already. There must be something else I can do."

Grandpa Charlie pulled a cigarette out of his shirt pocket. He lit it and stared out into the dark for a while. He stared so long that Emerson wondered if Grandpa had forgotten his question. Finally his grandfather said, "Did you notice the **dibe bighans** smell pretty bad?"

Emerson's shoulders slumped. *He changed the subject. No fair.* Then he sighed and held his nose between his fingers. "We're lucky the wind didn't blow this way."

"Tomorrow, as soon as the **dibe** leave the first **bighan**, you can take a bucket and shovel and clean up their droppings."

Emerson's plate clanged to the ground. "WHAT? You want me to pick up their poop?"

Grandpa Charlie nodded. "You can work on it a little every day. Perhaps next week I will leave you at

68

camp for a whole day so you can do a good job cleaning it up."

Emerson jumped up, stomped over to the footlocker and threw his plate and fork inside.

"Don't forget to close the lid."

Emerson turned back in a fury and slammed the lid shut. "I hate this place! I hate it! I hate it! I hate it!" He turned and looked for the sheep dogs. He saw them guarding the **dibe bighans**, and he ran toward them.

"Red, Flint," he called, and they pranced to meet him. He crouched in front of them and hugged their necks.

"I gotta get out of here," he told them. "This is all you know, so you don't understand. But I hate it! And now Grandpa's making me pick up sheep poop."

A coyote wailed in the distance, and the dogs bounded back to the **dibe bighans**. Emerson grunted. *They're too busy guarding **dibe** to have fun with me. I wish I had my own dog. At least I'd have a friend here.*

The next morning Emerson groaned, rolling out of his sleeping bag. First he scooped kibble for the dogs' breakfast. Then he dragged himself to the campfire. When he sat on the log to eat, he saw a metal bucket and shovel lying there. He groaned again. *Me and my big mouth. I'll never talk to Grandpa again. Never. Not unless I have to. I mean I REALLY have to. Like I'm DYING or something.*

When he finished breakfast, Emerson opened a footlocker and tossed his plate and fork inside. He opened

69

the other one and took out the candy sack. Just then his grandfather called for him to begin shoveling. Emerson shoved the candy in his pocket and picked up the bucket and shovel. Then he trudged over to the first *dibe bighan*.

"Aw, geez," Emerson grumbled. He breathed through his mouth so he wouldn't smell the sheep droppings. He half lifted, half dragged the bucket to a spot a short distance away. He dumped it and trudged back to the *bighan*. *Grandpa's over there with the dibe, pretending not to watch me. But I know he really is. I bet he's laughing, too.*

Emerson finished dumping the second bucket when his grandfather called his name.

"That's enough for now. Come quick. The *dibe* are moving." Grandpa Charlie turned to follow the herd. Emerson took his time catching up, and even then, he trailed behind. He wanted his grandfather to know that he was mad, really, really mad.

About mid-morning they stopped to let the *dibe* graze. Emerson felt the sun slide behind a cloud and looked up. A few gray clouds moved toward them.

A few hours later, Grandpa Charlie called Emerson to his side. "We'll start back for camp now." He pointed to the sky. "Those clouds are lower and darker now. The wind may blow them past us. Often on the Rez that happens. We think it will rain, but it does not." Then he whistled to the dogs to turn the *dibe* around.

Halfway back to camp it began to rain. The dogs

worked to keep the *dibe* together, but thunder frightened some of them. Grandpa Charlie kept watch farther ahead.

Emerson bent his head down and pushed forward, rain dripping off the brim of his hat. He was soaked to the skin, and his feet sloshed in his boots. A clash of thunder and lightning startled a mother *dibe* and lamb. They bolted right in front of him, running away from the herd. "Grandpa!" he yelled, but his grandfather did not hear him.

"Oh great," he moaned. He looked for Red and Flint but didn't see them. The mother and lamb had slowed down but were still moving away from the herd. "I guess it's up to me," he muttered and ran toward them.

"Hyah! Hyah!" Emerson yelled, waving his arms. The mother darted away from him, but the lamb stood still, as if afraid to move. He bent and picked it up.

Emerson faced the mother. "Look! I have your baby! Better come get her!" Then he turned and sloshed back toward the herd. Seconds later the mother caught up and walked by his side. He grinned. *I knew she wouldn't leave her baby. I'm so smart.*

Emerson reached the herd and put the lamb on the ground. Backing away, he looked around for his grandfather. *Did he see me do something good? Something right?* But Grandpa Charlie's back was turned to him. *I guess not.* Emerson trudged on with the herd. The rain let up to a light drizzle.

By the time they reached camp, sunlight shone

through the clouds. Emerson ran ahead to open the ***dibe bighan*** gates while Grandpa Charlie and the dogs herded the dibe inside them. Finally the last gate was shut. His grandfather said, "Gather some wood. A fire will help us dry out."

Emerson threw back the tarp covering the woodpile and pulled out a few branches. When he returned to the campfire, he saw his grandfather standing still, staring at the footlockers.

Emerson's eyes popped wide open. *The lids! Oh no! I forgot to close them!*

He dropped the wood and joined his grandfather. The footlocker holding canned food, pots and plates had standing water. But the other one was a soggy mess of water-logged flour, corn meal, sugar, salt, toilet paper — everything was ruined.

Emerson turned to look at the dogs' food bin. *Where's that lid?* His heart sank when he saw it resting on the ground. He shuffled over to look inside, and his stomach flip-flopped. *It's all mush.*

He looked over at his grandfather, afraid of what would happen next. His mouth felt dry, like he'd been running up and down the soccer field all day. "Grandpa?" He waited a moment, then started toward him. "Grandpa, I'm sorry. I didn't mean to forget."

Grandpa Charlie waved him away with his hand, his voice angry. "Do you see what you have done? You do not think. You do not care. You only feel sorry for yourself."

He bent to pick up the dropped wood and started a fire.

Emerson stood still. *Man, I really messed up. Now what do I do?* He shifted his weight back and forth, afraid to move.

When the fire caught, Grandpa Charlie leaned over a footlocker and pulled out a can of pinto beans and a can of peaches. "This will be dinner. You can watch the beans cook while I drive to the road and call Sam. If he can watch the *dibe* tomorrow, we'll go to Bobcat Ridge for new supplies." He frowned at Emerson. "You must go with me. I cannot trust you alone with the *dibe*."

Emerson took a step toward his grandfather. "Grandpa?" His voice shook. "I said I was sorry."

Grandpa Charlie looked hard at him. "You disappoint me, *Shi Tsoi.* Very much. I expect my daughter's son to have more sense, to take more pride in what he does." He waved Emerson toward the dogs' food bin. "Scoop some of that mess for the dogs. They are hungry. You can tell THEM you are sorry."

Emerson bowed his head, tears burning his eyes. He scooped the mushy food for Red and Flint and put their dishes on the ground. Both dogs sniffed at their bowls and looked up at Emerson. Then they slowly began lapping it up.

He knelt and watched them while they ate. "I'm really sorry," he whispered. "We'll get more food for you tomorrow." He looked over his shoulder at his grandfather dumping beans into a pot. "I just don't belong out here.

It's all wrong." He lowered his voice to a whisper. "When I get to town, I'll sneak away." He bit his lip. "It might be my last chance."

11

This Dog Is Mine!

 Emerson fidgeted in his grandfather's truck, watching Sam and the dogs lead the *dibe* away. Grandpa Charlie inspected everything in camp before sliding into the driver's seat. He started the engine without a word.

They rode in silence. *Grandpa's still mad at me. I told him I was sorry. He should have said it's all right, but he didn't.* Emerson looked out the window. *Wonder how long it'll take me to walk from Bobcat Ridge to Gallup? Maybe somebody will pick me up. I'll call Mom when I get to Gallup. She'll come get me.*

Sitting back in his seat, it was easy to imagine all the fun things he'd do when he got home. *I sure won't miss this place.* He thought for a moment. *Well, I'll miss Red and Flint. They're fun to play with. I'll ask Mom to get me a dog.* He smiled as he imagined playing fetch and chase. *Yeah, that's what I want when I get home, my very own dog.*

It seemed like hours before the sign that said Bobcat Ridge appeared. Grandpa Charlie pulled into the trading post, parked in front and honked the horn. This time, Emerson waited for his grandfather to get out.

Emerson jumped down and closed his door. Carefully, he looked around and noticed two buildings to the left of the trading post. *Not too far, just a short run. I can sneak off and hide when he's not looking.*

Grandpa Charlie stopped at the trading post steps. "Emerson, hurry up."

Muffling a grunt, Emerson shuffled toward his grandfather. Suddenly, a movement caught his eye. Something crawled out from under the porch. Emerson stared a moment before realizing what it was.

"A dog! Grandpa, look." He ran toward it and knelt, patting his legs. The dog hesitated a moment, then crept slowly to him.

Grandpa Charlie shook his head. "Leave it alone and come with me." He started up the steps.

Emerson ignored him and let the dog creep into his lap. "Poor little dog," he whispered while he petted her. "You're so dirty. Where's your collar? You must be lost."

The dog whimpered softly and nuzzled Emerson's hand. Her big brown eyes looked up into his, and Emerson knew at once he was meant to find her. He'd wanted his own dog ever since he got to the Rez. She wasn't the big

shepherd type dog he imagined, but that didn't matter now. She was all alone, lost in a strange place, just like him. She put her paws on his chest and licked his chin. He made up his mind to keep her.

"Emerson! Come now." Grandpa Charlie's voice was stern.

Emerson glanced at his grandfather standing on the porch. Then he looked back down at the little dog. "Don't worry." He petted her head and ears. "You're not alone anymore. You're my dog now, and I'll take care of you." He scooped her into his arms and carried her to his grandfather.

"Look, Grandpa. It's a wiener dog, a girl wiener dog. I can tell she's lost, so she needs a home. She's my dog now."

Grandpa Charlie frowned. "Emerson, we do not keep dogs for pets. This one is useless at sheep camp. It will not survive. Leave it here."

"What? But she's all alone." The dog wagged her tail and licked his chin again.

"I said no." Grandpa Charlie's voice was firm. "Put it down. If it has no owner, someone else will take it." He grasped Emerson's shoulder.

Emerson jerked away. "You don't want me to be happy. You just want me to hate being stuck here with you."

"Emerson, put the dog down." His grandfather's voice deepened. "Now."

Very slowly, Emerson set her on the ground. *I can make him change his mind. I just have to think of the right words.* The dog danced at his feet while Emerson stomped up the steps. When the screen door opened, she darted through. But Grandpa Charlie caught her.

"Dogs belong outside." He set her on the porch and closed the door behind him.

Emerson knelt inside and looked at her through the screen. "I'm sorry, little dog." He heard Grandpa Charlie call so he glanced over his shoulder. His grandfather motioned for him to join him.

Emerson shook his head and turned back to the dog. "I'll talk to you while Grandpa's busy. Come closer so I can pet you through the screen door. You sure are cute, but you need someone to take care of you. Where did you come from?"

"*Ya'at'eeh*, Charlie." He heard Jolene's voice. "Back so soon? Emerson must eat a lot."

Emerson looked over his shoulder. His grandfather leaned sideways against the counter, still eyeing him.

"*Ya'at'eeh*, Jolene. Yesterday's rain ruined much of our food and the dogs' food." He looked over his shoulder at Emerson. "My grandson forgot to close the lids."

Oh great! Emerson glared at his grandfather. *Why not tell the whole world what I did?*

"That's a shame." She waved at Emerson. "Looks like he found himself a friend. Tourists left her here yesterday. Haven't heard from them, and they haven't

79

come back. Strange they didn't notice she was gone." Jolene shrugged. "Sweet little dog, but I don't need another mouth to feed. You can take her."

Grandpa Charlie shook his head. "I cannot take a dog like that to sheep camp. You know what may happen to it."

She sighed. "Well, you're probably right. Too bad, though."

They began talking about supplies, and Emerson stopped listening. "Your family left you behind?" he whispered. "I knew you were lost when I saw you. We're the same, you and me. I'm lost, too, sort of. Mom left me with my grandpa over there." The dog pressed her body against the screen. "But I have no friends, just like you."

Glancing up, he saw Grandpa Charlie still looking at him. He turned back to his dog. "He's watching me. He's always watching me." Emerson whispered. "I'm running away, just as soon as he turns his back. I'm taking you with me."

He heard someone walking up behind him and climbed to his feet. Jolene handed over a Tootsie Roll Pop. "Your grandfather said it was okay."

Emerson thanked her and stuffed it in his shirt pocket. "I wish I could have this dog," he said quietly. "Those people shouldn't have left her."

"I know," Jolene replied. "I wish you could have her, too." She ruffled his hair. "Don't worry. I'll find a good home for her."

Emerson watched her walk back to the counter. He turned to the dog and whispered. "You're not going to another home. You're coming with me." He looked back at the counter. Jolene was packing boxes, and his grandfather turned his back to look at something on a shelf.

"Now's my chance!" Emerson whispered. Quietly he opened the screen door just enough to slip through. Then he picked up the dog and tiptoed down the steps.

"Don't be scared." Emerson began to run. "We're gonna hide in that building over there."

He'd taken only a few steps when he heard Grandpa Charlie yell, "Emerson! Stop!"

Emerson looked back and only hesitated a second. *No! I won't stop.* He held his dog tight to his chest and ran for the building.

12

Grandpa Gives In

In seconds Grandpa Charlie caught up and jerked him to a stop. "Where are you going?"

Emerson's voice trembled. "I'm running away with my dog." Defiantly, he looked his grandfather in the eyes.

The old man glanced away and let go of Emerson's shoulder. "You cannot run away."

"Then let me keep my dog. I know she's lost. I heard the lady say so. She needs me. Please, I'll take care of her."

"No, Emerson. That is a *bilagaana* dog. Do you know what that means?"

Puzzled, Emerson shook his head. Those kids at the Chapter House called him a *bilagaana*. Could a dog be one, too?

"It means a city dog, a white people's dog. It does

83

not belong at sheep camp."

"Then I don't belong there, either," Emerson snapped back. "I'm a **bilagaana**, too. Those boys at the Chapter House said so."

Grandpa Charlie sighed deeply. "That is different. You're my grandson, and I'll take care of you. It's wrong to take a dog like this to camp. It will be lured away by **ma'ii**, coyotes, and eaten. Do not ask me again."

A lump rose in Emerson's throat. "Why are you being so mean? I hate it here! And I hate you!" He stood his ground and did not move.

Grandpa Charlie ignored the comment. He grasped Emerson's shoulder and guided him to the truck. Jolene stood beside it, the box of supplies at her feet.

"**Shi Tsoi**, put the dog down and get in," he said.

"You can't do this!" Emerson's voice cracked. "I'll tell Mom. And she'll never forgive you! Never!" He held tight to his dog.

His grandfather sighed and bent down on one knee. Slowly he smoothed the hair back from Emerson's forehead. "I am sorry, **Shi Tsoi**." His grandfather's voice was quiet and gentle. "I know you want this dog, but the mesa is too dangerous for city dogs. It will be safer here."

Emerson was used to doing what adults told him, even when he didn't like it. Tears filled his eyes, and he set the dog on the ground. "I'm sorry, girl," he whispered, patting her head.

Jolene picked up the dog and backed away.

Grandpa Charlie lifted the supplies and set them in the bed of the truck. Then he opened the door for Emerson and walked around to the other side.

Emerson slid into the seat and slammed the door. Grandpa Charlie started the engine and pulled out of the parking area.

Sudden shrill barks split the air. Quickly Emerson scooted over to look out the window. He saw the dog twist out of Jolene's arms and jump to the ground. Ears flapping, she bolted into the road. "Grandpa! The dog's running after us."

Grandpa Charlie looked out his side mirror and scowled. "Fool dog! Get out of the road!"

Emerson's heart sank watching the dog fall farther and farther behind. He turned and clutched his grandfather's arm. "Stop, Grandpa! Stop! I can't leave her! I can't!" Emerson's throat felt so tight it hurt. "I'm all alone here. I have no friends. Please stop, Grandpa. Please!"

With a grunt, the old man hit the brakes and the truck lurched to a bumpy stop. Emerson jumped out and ran back to the panting dog. Gently he picked her up and carried her to the truck.

"Thank you, Grandpa!" He climbed in and slammed the door. "We belong together, I just know it. I'll take good care of her, I promise. You won't be sorry." His face beamed while the little dog licked his ear and nose. He squeezed her tighter to his chest.

Grandpa Charlie exhaled loudly and shook his head. "I am already sorry," he muttered and eased the truck back onto the highway.

Emerson smiled, rubbing his cheek on the dog's head. "What shall I name you?" He glanced at his grandfather. *Maybe I should be nicer to him. He's letting me keep her.* "What's a good name for a wiener dog, Grandpa?"

His grandfather shrugged and did not answer. Emerson leaned back in the seat and thought. It had to be the perfect name. "I know! I'll call you Lucky, because today's our lucky day." He turned to his grandfather. "You think that's a good name, Grandpa?"

Grandpa Charlie glanced over at the dog but said nothing.

Emerson shook his head. It didn't matter. He wasn't alone anymore. Lucky curled up on his lap and closed her eyes.

My very own dog. My new best friend. Man, are we gonna have fun! He yawned. *Maybe now I'll make it through this awful summer.* He felt tired, like he'd played a hard soccer game. Slowly his eyes closed.

Grandpa Charlie looked at the long stretch of road ahead of them. It bothered him that Emerson begged for the dog. Each time his grandson said "please," he cringed. *This is not the way of the **Diné**. We do not beg. I have much to teach him, if he is willing to learn.*

He glanced down at this grandson. *I've lived alone for too long. I got used to it. Now **Shi Tsoi** is changing my life. Maybe, like him, I am lonely, too.*

The old man listened to the sounds of breathing as they grew slower and quieter. *They are both asleep.* He shifted his attention back to the road and gripped the steering wheel. *I am afraid this summer with **Shi Tsoi** will not be easy for me. Or for him.*

13

Lucky Spooks the Sheep

Emerson woke up when the truck turned down a bumpy road. *Aha! Now I know where I am.* He recognized the roads and paths leading back to sheep camp. As they rolled to a stop, Lucky poked her head out the window and snorted.

Grandpa Charlie got out, followed by Emerson holding Lucky. The moment he set her on the ground, she began scampering around and sniffing.

"Keep an eye on her while we work," his grandfather warned. "First, we'll clean out the footlockers and dry them. Then you can stock the new food supplies while I rehang that gate on the ***dibe bighan***."

Emerson started to work. But every time he took his eyes off Lucky, she got into trouble. First she dug in the ashes from the campfire, kicking ashes everywhere.

"No, Lucky," Emerson wiped ashes from her nose

and paws. "Don't dig!" After putting her down, he emptied the cooking pans, forks and spoons from the footlocker. He heard her snuffle through the things on the ground, but paid no attention.

With a grunt he overturned the footlocker to drain the water. He heard funny sounds and looked behind him. Lucky was chewing on a wood spoon. It was already splintered.

"No, Lucky!" He pulled the spoon out of her mouth. "Bad dog!"

Her tail tucked between her legs, the little dog lowered her head.

"Aw, I'm sorry," Emerson picked her up to pet her. "All this is new. You don't know any better." He set her on the ground. "Stay there." He glanced at his grandfather. *He's frowning. I bet he saw everything she did.*

Grandpa Charlie finished emptying the other footlocker and left to fix the gate. Emerson began drying his footlocker with a towel when he heard shredding sounds. He looked over his shoulder.

"Lucky, no!" He jumped up and grabbed what was left of a sack from her mouth. She'd scattered hardened chunks of cornmeal all over. He pried open her mouth. "No, don't eat this stuff." She swallowed quickly before he could pull a chunk from her mouth.

Emerson picked her up and set her right in front of him. "Stay here," he said, his voice stern. "Lay down. I mean it. No more trouble."

She lay down and watched him. He took some of the new supplies from the box and put them inside the clean footlocker. When he glanced at Lucky, her muzzle rested on her front paws, and her eyes were closed.

Aw, look at her. She's taking a nap. He turned his back and lifted the flour sack from the box. He stopped to watch his grandfather work on the gate. *I bet I can learn that,* he thought. Suddenly, Emerson heard scratching sounds. Spinning around, he caught Lucky, head first, inside the footlocker. Her tail wagged like crazy while she scratched a hole in the sack of sugar.

"No! No! No!" He lifted her out. "Bad dog. Bad dog. That's people food." He set her down and she rolled over on her back, paws in the air, whimpering. She looked so sorry that he felt guilty for yelling at her. "Here, get up. It's okay."

Emerson set her on her feet and coaxed her to the sleeping shelter. "Lay down. Take a nap." She curled up on his sleeping bag and closed her eyes. "Good dog. There's nothing in here you can hurt."

He was almost done with his work when Grandpa Charlie walked up to him. He held a piece of rope in his hands. "Here, tie up your dog." He nodded toward the sleeping shelter. "It's chewing your sleeping bag."

Emerson spun around and sprinted to the shelter. Lucky lay on his sleeping bag holding fabric between her front paws. He could already see a small wet hole. She jumped up and wagged her tail, like she was ready to play.

Emerson groaned and picked her up. "Why are you so bad? Why?"

Lucky's tail stopped wagging and she shoved her head under his armpit.

Emerson walked back to his grandfather and took the rope.

"Tie the dog to the bumper. Any more trouble, it'll go back to the trading post." Grandpa Charlie walked back to the *dibe bighan*.

Emerson sucked his breath between his teeth. "Lucky, you have to be good, you hear?" Just then he heard a whistle. Looking up, he saw Sam and the *dibe* coming over the hill.

"I know, let's go watch. That way you can get used to the *dibe*. I'll tie you up later."

Emerson shuffled her to his other arm and walked toward the first *bighan*. The *dibe* crowded around, kicking up large clouds of dust.

Flint darted nearby rounding up a straggling *dibe*. Lucky tensed and growled. Flint loped closer and she began squirming in Emerson's arms. He looked down at her. "Hey, girl, what's wrong?"

Then Flint ran right in front of them. Lucky jerked free and thudded to the ground. Emerson bent to grab her, but she scrambled to her feet and chased after Flint, barking. Instantly she was lost among the dust and the *dibe*.

"Lucky! Come back!" Emerson plunged forward, looking left and right. Her shrill barks startled the sheep, and they scattered everywhere. Some ran back out the open gate.

"What's happening?" Grandpa Charlie's voice roared above the noise. "Get that dog out of there!"

Emerson pushed his way into the *bighan*. *I have to find her before they trample her.* The swirling dust stung his eyes and throat, and he began to cough. Half shielding his eyes and nose with his arm, Emerson stumbled through the sheep.

He heard a sharp cry and stopped just in time. Lucky cowered in the dust at his feet, whimpering. Emerson picked her up, holding her close to his chest.

"It's okay. You're safe. I have you," he said. Lucky trembled in his arms while Emerson waded through the sheep, looking for the opening.

Grandpa Charlie met them at the gate.

"Take that dog and tie it to the truck." The old man's voice stretched tight with anger. "Stay there until I come for you. Do not disobey me again." He turned and strode back to the *dibe bighan*, waving his rope at the herd.

Emerson carried Lucky back to the truck. "Maybe bringing you here *was* a mistake," he said. "You don't belong here, anymore than me." He set her on the ground and tied her to the truck.

Lucky's wide brown eyes looked up at him and her tail thumped against the ground.

"You didn't mean to make trouble. I know that. But Grandpa looks like he's really mad."

A horrible thought hit him. "He said one more problem and he'd send you back. But he can't!" He hugged his dog. "You'll get used to all this. Besides, you're my only friend out here. You need me to take care of you."

Emerson sat next to Lucky and watched the sheepdogs work. "What if...?" His mind began to tick. "What if you could learn to herd sheep, like Red and Flint?" Emerson grinned. "Yeah. I'll tell Grandpa we'll teach you to be a sheepdog. Then he'll let you stay." Pleased with his idea, Emerson leaned back against the front tire. "We'll talk to Grandpa about training you."

When the *dibe* were counted and penned, Grandpa Charlie walked back to the truck. "Come and help with dinner."

Emerson stood up. "What about Lucky? She didn't mean to do anything bad."

Grandpa Charlie ignored his comment. "Red and Flint are hungry and must be fed. You can feed that one too." He frowned at Lucky. "Tomorrow it goes back to the trading post."

"No, Grandpa!" Emerson's face flushed. "You can't do that! Give her another chance!"

Grandpa Charlie turned his back and walked away.

14
Little Dog in a Big Mesa
(Lucky)

Don't take me back! Lucky pawed her boy's sleeve. *I'll be good. I promise.*

"Stay here. Don't worry." Emerson whispered. "If I do what he says, it might be easier to change his mind." He bent and petted her before following his grandfather.

Lucky's stomach rumbled. *Hurry back with dinner. I'm starved!* She watched Emerson so closely she didn't hear the sheepdogs walk up behind her.

"Hah! This little squirt caused all that trouble?"

Startled, she twirled around and faced the lean black dog.

"What are you?" He circled her, sniffing. "You can't be a dog. You're deformed! What happened to your legs?"

"I am not deformed!" Lucky growled and arched her tail over her back. "I am a dachshund." Proudly

95

she puffed out her chest. "We're built this way to hunt badgers."

"You're a badger hunter?" The older red dog appeared interested. "A *nahashch'id*?"

"She's no *nahashch'id*. She's too stupid." The black dog pushed her with his paw. "Why'd you bark at the *dibe*?"

"*Dibe*? You mean those sheep? I didn't bark at them." She arched her neck to stare up at him. "I barked at you. You came too close to my boy, so I chased you away."

"Don't be silly." The black dog towered over her. "You're too little to chase anything away."

Lucky growled. "I'm a great watchdog. I protected my first family. I guarded my house and yard, too."

"You lived in a house?" The red dog sat next to her. "I did, too, a long time ago."

Lucky sniffed his nose. *This dog seems nice. Not mean like the other one.* "Yes," she said with pride. "No one broke in while I was on guard. Dachshunds are fierce fighters."

The black dog sneered. "Well, you didn't look so fierce today in the *dibe bighan*. You cowered in the dirt. That boy had to save you."

Lucky lowered her head in shame. *I was so scared. Those hooves stomped all around me. I didn't know where to run. And even worse, they all saw my fear.* Her head sank so low her nose touched the ground.

The old dog nudged her neck. "Pay no attention to Flint. I used to be a dog like you." His voice was kind, and Lucky raised her head to look at him.

"When I was a pup, Charlie found me on a street and brought me to the reservation. He named me Red and taught me to herd sheep." He pointed his nose at Flint. "Charlie and I worked together for many years before Flint showed up. He still had his baby teeth."

Flint nodded. "I remember, Red. You taught me to herd sheep."

Lucky looked over at the **dibe bighans**. "Is it hard to learn? Maybe I can be a sheepdog, too."

Flint snorted, "With those stumpy legs? You're kidding me."

Red stood and took a step forward. "Stop it, Flint."

The black dog looked away for a moment. Then he backed up and sat down.

Red turned to Lucky. "You must learn to be useful, like us. Tomorrow, if you're still alive, I'll start teaching you."

Lucky's legs stiffened. That didn't sound good. "What do you mean, if I'm still alive?"

"Here on the mesa, small animals have many enemies." Red cocked his head. "Like owls and hawks. They dive from the sky to catch and eat their prey. They'll think you're just a strange looking rabbit, a **gah**. If you see them, hide quickly. Or run to the humans."

"Tell her about the **ch'iidii**," Flint interrupted.

"That'll scare her."

Lucky began trembling. This sounded bad. "*Ch'iidii*? What are they?"

"Creatures something like us. The humans call them *ma'ii* or coyotes. They hunt small animals for food and sing strange, beautiful songs at night. If they lure you away from safety, they will eat you."

"Eat me?" Lucky crept close to Red and leaned against his legs. "What should I do?"

"Stay close to the humans," he cautioned her, "and to the fire. The *ch'iidii* don't come close to camp. At least not usually."

Her body began trembling again. "Why do you call them *ch'iidii*?"

"Their eyes are different from ours," Flint answered. "Makes them look like evil spirits. That's what *ch'iidii* means. Evil spirits."

"Yes," Red nodded. "Bark loud if you see them. Then run away! Never follow them into the mesa if they sing to you."

The dogs turned at the sound of footsteps. Emerson walked up carrying bowls of food and water. "Red, Flint. Your dinner is over there." He pointed his chin toward the water tanks.

Red and Flint scampered off, and Emerson put the bowls on the ground. Then he sat next to Lucky. She wolfed down her food and lapped up half her bowl of water. With belly full, she crawled into his lap.

This is a nice boy, like the one in my first family. I was happy there. Maybe I can be happy here. Lucky pawed her boy's arm. "I learned about ***ch'iidii*** and owls and how to stay alive." She wagged her tail. "And tomorrow Red's going to teach me to be a sheepdog, like him."

But it seemed like Emerson didn't hear a word she said. *Why don't humans understand their dogs? Dogs always understand their humans.*

Emerson petted Lucky. "Something has to happen so Grandpa can't take you back. I told him he should change his mind. He has to give you another chance. Mom would, if she was here."

Lucky pawed her boy's chest. "Tell him I'm going to be a sheepdog. Then I'll be just like Red and Flint."

Emerson climbed to his feet. "Sam is staying overnight. He's nice to me, so I'll go help him fix dinner. But I'll be back. You can sleep with me tonight in the sleeping bag. You know, the one you chewed."

He folded his arms across his chest. "Now I remember the paths to get to the highway." Emerson frowned and shook his head. "If Grandpa doesn't change his mind, we'll walk back to the trading post. That nice lady would let me call Mom. Then Grandpa will be sorry."

Lucky watched Emerson head back to the campfire. *He's my boy now, and I'm his dog. We can have fun, like with my first boy.* She shivered. *Not like that second boy. He was horrible, and so was his family. I'm glad I ran away.*

She stretched out on the ground and rested her muzzle on her paws. Emerson looked so far away, and she felt so alone. She blinked at the sky. The sun almost touched the ground, and soon it would be dark. She remembered the story of the *ch'iidii* and whimpered softly.

I've never been eaten before, but I'm pretty sure it would hurt. She raised her head and watched Emerson help his grandfather. *Dachshunds are fierce fighters,* she reminded herself. But she wished she was closer to the campfire.

15
From Bad to Worse

The next morning, Emerson woke suddenly and sniffed the air. *Grandpa's cooking fry bread!* His mouth began to water and he sat up. Lucky burrowed out from the sleeping bag. Sniffing the air, she growled in the direction of the sheep. Quickly Emerson clamped his hand over her muzzle. "No, don't do that," he whispered.

He heard footsteps coming toward him and scooted out of the sleeping bag. Grandpa Charlie waved to him.

"Get dressed and come eat." The old man glanced at Lucky and shook his head in warning. "Tie that dog up before she causes more trouble."

Oh man. Even in the morning he's grumpy and mean. Emerson dressed and tied Lucky to the truck bumper. "Wait here. I'll make Grandpa change his mind about you. I promise."

He turned to leave, but Lucky pulled hard at the end of the rope and began choking. "No, Lucky!" Emerson grabbed her. "Stop!" Carefully, he retied the rope so it hung loose around her neck.

"Stay put. It'll be okay." He turned to leave and saw Red wander over. Emerson smiled, watching Lucky sniff noses with him.

She's making friends with Red, and he's the head honcho! Grandpa has to let her stay. Emerson walked over to the campfire and sat down with the older men.

He didn't know much about Sam. He was Grandpa's friend and helped out when Grandpa Charlie had to be away. Now they each greeted Emerson with a nod.

Sam poured coffee in a tin cup. "You drink coffee, boy?"

Surprised, Emerson shook his head. "No, Dad says I'm too young."

Sam glanced at Grandpa Charlie, who nodded.

"You look old enough." Sam stirred in powdered cream and sugar. Then he handed the cup to Emerson.

Wrinkling his nose, Emerson blew into the hot coffee. *Wow! If Zach could see me now! No one in my class drinks coffee yet.* He took a small sip and swallowed. *Ugh!* He looked up at Sam.

"It needs to be sweeter. Can I have more sugar?"

Sam handed over the sugar canister. Emerson turned it upside down and sugar poured into his cup.

Grandpa Charlie snatched it from his hand.

"Enough." He handed his grandson a plastic spoon.

Carefully, Emerson stirred his coffee and took another sip. A happy smile spread across his face. "Now this tastes good. Kind of like a hot coffee milkshake." Grandpa Charlie handed him a plate of fry bread with beans and chile. "What a great breakfast, Grandpa. Much better than boring old cereal." *That'll put me on Grandpa's good side,* Emerson thought. *Besides, it's true.*

While he ate, Emerson watched Lucky play with Red. She darted to the end of her rope while Red chased her. Emerson smiled. *Maybe this summer will be okay with Lucky here. At least we can play together and have some fun. She knows what it's like to be left behind.* His heart hammered a little, and he took a deep breath. It was now or never.

"Look at Lucky, Grandpa! She's playing with the other dogs. She's getting used to the sheep. She didn't bark once this morning." He smiled, nodding his head up and down. "I bet we can train her to be a sheepdog."

Grandpa Charlie set his plate on the ground. "Emerson, you and I will herd the **dibe** to pasture. After we leave, Sam will take the dog back to the trading post."

"No, Grandpa!" He scooted closer to his grandfather. "Give her another chance. Please? She's being good. And we can teach her to herd sheep." His voice trembled. "Mom would give her another chance."

The old man's face grew stern. "Your mother is not here." He tossed the rest of his coffee on the campfire.

103

"Today we herd the *dibe* farther away, so we'll take the horses. Come with me." He stood and motioned Emerson to follow.

Emerson felt cold and numb inside. *Think! Think! I can't lose Lucky!* He followed his grandfather, trying to form magic words to change the old man's mind.

"Grandpa, she'll be scared by herself. What if she doesn't find a home? If she's not a good sheepdog, we can leave her in camp all day. I'll take care of her at night. Please, Grandpa."

Grandpa Charlie didn't answer. He approached the first horse and spoke softly to it in words Emerson couldn't understand. He motioned for Emerson to come close.

"This is my horse. Watch while I saddle him."

"No!" Emerson snapped. "I don't care about your old horse!" He tugged his grandfather's arm. "Why won't you listen to me?"

Grandpa Charlie pulled his arm away. He picked up a saddle and placed it on his horse. "Watch how I cinch this," was all he said.

Emerson turned away. *I'll grab Lucky, and we'll just leave. I can get to the highway.* He took a step toward the truck, then stopped, puzzled. *I don't see her.* He saw Red and Flint standing by the *dibe bighans*. *Maybe she crawled under the truck.*

Squinting against the sun, he saw the rope still tied to the bumper. He shaded his glasses with his hand for a better look. His eyes traveled from the bumper down the rope to the other end lying on the ground.

Lucky was gone!

16
Lying to Grandpa

"Emerson!" Startled, he turned back to his grandfather.

"We'll saddle the pinto now." Grandpa Charlie threw a saddle blanket over the horse's back, but Emerson couldn't pay attention.

Where's Lucky? Did she know Sam was coming for her? Maybe she's hiding. He rubbed his forehead. *What if she's in trouble?* He glanced at his grandfather. *I should tell Grandpa. Maybe he'd help me find her. No, wait! If they find Lucky, Sam will take her away.* He stared miserably at the ground. *What should I do? Think! Think!*

"Emerson!" He looked up at his grandfather. "Are you still asleep? You did not pay attention."

Emerson's eyes flicked to the saddled pinto. "What was that, Grandpa?"

107

"I said: do you know how to ride a horse?"

He hesitated, then nodded. "Once Mom took me to place where they rent horses," he mumbled.

"Then you don't know how to ride. I will teach you. Come over to my side."

Emerson glanced back at the rope lying on the ground. *She has to be hiding. But where? Under the truck?* He walked around to his grandfather like he was in a bad dream.

Grandpa Charlie boosted Emerson up onto the pinto. "Hold on to the saddle horn with both hands." He waited until Emerson grasped it. Then he turned to mount his own horse.

Emerson looked back at the **dibe bighans**. They were all empty, and the dogs were herding the flock north. Sam waved to Grandpa Charlie and walked over to the truck.

"I will lead your horse until you're comfortable." Grandpa Charlie held the reins to the pinto in one hand, and both horses moved forward.

Emerson's mind raced desperately. *He'll see she's gone. First place he'll look is under the truck.* He turned toward his grandfather. "Grandpa, don't send Lucky back."

The old man ignored his plea. "We'll begin your riding lessons when we reach flatter ground."

Emerson listened as if in a dream. *It's happening too fast!* He looked over his shoulder and saw Sam kneel on the ground to look under the truck.

Please don't find Lucky, he prayed silently.

"Emerson!" Grandpa Charlie's voice was sharper than usual.

Twisting around, Emerson clung to the saddle horn and leaned toward his grandfather. "Grandpa, please can't — "

"No," Grandpa Charlie held up his hand. "Speak no more of the dog. Pay attention to your horse."

Emerson swayed in the saddle when the pinto moved forward. He looked over his shoulder and saw Sam carrying something under his arm. *No! He found her.* His eyes misted, and his stomach twisted in knots. He wanted to race back and rescue his dog, but his grandfather held the reins.

He wiped his eyes with his sleeve and glared at the old man's back. *If that's the way you want it, then I'll run back to the trading post tonight and get Lucky.* Anger boiled inside him. *We'll find someplace to live where people want us.*

Sam called out to Grandpa Charlie, and they stopped. Emerson turned to see the other man put down a sack and walk toward them. *A sack? It's only a sack!* Just then, Emerson heard a faint, shrill yip. His eyes darted around toward the rear of the flock. A small animal stood still, all by itself, as the sheep moved forward.

It's Lucky! She's hiding out in the sheep herd! Emerson was so amazed, he almost laughed out loud. She wagged her tail and quickly darted back into the herd.

Sam walked up and spoke to Grandpa Charlie. "Dog's gone. Slipped her rope."

Slowly Grandpa Charlie turned in his saddle to look at his grandson. Emerson dropped his eyes and looked down at his saddle horn.

"*Shi Tsoi,* do you know about this?" His voice was low.

Emerson looked up and words tumbled out. "Grandpa, she started to choke when I tied the rope, so I made it looser so she wouldn't get hurt. But I didn't untie her, so I guess she got away all by herself."

The old man's gaze was intense. "Do you know where she is?"

Emerson flushed and looked down at his saddle horn again. "Maybe she ran away," he mumbled.

Cautiously, he glanced up. Grandpa Charlie stood in his stirrups and swept the sheep herd with his eyes. He sat back in the saddle and was silent for a while. Finally, Emerson heard him sigh.

"Forget the dog, Sam. If you find it before you leave, take it to the trading post." Still holding the reins of the pinto, Grandpa Charlie flicked the reins of his own horse. Both horses moved forward to join the herd.

Emerson's grin spread from ear to ear. *Woo-hoo! Grandpa didn't see her! I'll save food from dinner tonight and sneak it to her. Maybe I can sneak her into my sleeping bag, too.*

He stared at his grandfather's back and felt a pang of guilt. Lying always made his stomach churn. He never lied to his dad. Whenever he lied to his mom, she always found out and gave him extra chores.

But this time Mom would understand, I know she would. But I hate feeling guilty. He thought for a minute. *I know. I'll ask Grandpa what herding was like when he was my age. It'll make him happy, and I'll feel better.* Emerson scowled and shrugged. *I'm stuck here for now, anyway.*

Then his thoughts brightened. He pictured himself playing fetch and tug of war with Lucky. What fun they'd have when she could finally come out of hiding!

Emerson nudged the pinto forward until he rode alongside his grandfather.

"What was it like, Grandpa, the first time you went to sheep camp?"

17

I'm a Nahashch'id

(Lucky)

 He thinks he's got me! Hah! Lucky leaned on her front paws, with her hind end up in the air and tail wagging. Red jumped toward her, and she darted to the end of her rope. The big dog chased after her. At the last second Lucky darted under his legs and almost bumped into Flint.

The black dog jumped out of her way. "Watch it, Squirt." He bumped her as he walked past. "Hey, Red. Want to hear something important?"

Red stood still. "Go ahead."

"Charlie and Sam talked about getting rid of her." He pointed his nose at Lucky.

Red cocked his head. "What exactly did you hear?"

Flint yawned widely and stretched his lean body. "Charlie told Sam to wait until they take the *dibe* to graze. Then he's supposed to take our ***nahashch'id*** back to the trading post."

"No!" Lucky cried. "He can't do that. I have to stay with my boy. He needs me." She turned to Red. "I have to hide before Sam gets here. But I'm tied up. What'll I do?"

Red bit into the rope around her neck and tugged. "Rope's loose. Back up until it's tight."

Lucky turned around so she faced the truck bumper. Steadily, she backed up until the loop came to the top of her head.

"Now pull! And shake your head back and forth." Red urged. "Harder. See if the rope slips off."

Lucky shook her head back and forth. The rope slipped forward over her ears and off her nose. She was free!

"Quick!" Red urged. "Crawl under the truck to the other side. Then run behind that brush pile near the last ***dibe bighan***. Stay there till I come for you."

Lucky spun around, ran under the truck, and raced for the brush pile. She skidded to a stop behind the cut branches. Slowly she stuck out her head and peeked around.

Flint and Red walked over to the first ***dibe bighan*** and stood, ready to work. She risked poking her head out farther and saw Emerson staring at the truck. *Uh oh, he sees I'm gone.* Then his grandfather called him, and he turned away. Quickly she ducked back.

My boy's worried. Lucky paced back and forth behind the brush pile. *But I have to stay here. I promised Red.*

Just then she heard whistles and the sounds of *dibe* crowding out of the first *bighan*. She listened while the gates to the second and third ones opened. Then she heard dog paws rushing toward her.

Red darted around the brush pile. "Quick! Follow me to the middle of the herd. Stay there, and you'll be safe. Don't walk to the edge of the herd. Charlie might see you."

Red spun around, and Lucky dashed after him. In an instant she was surrounded by *dibe*, and she plowed to a stop. *They're big as mountains!* She struggled against the urge to bark. *They almost trampled me yesterday. Horrible, horrible beasts!* Her heart thumped inside her chest.

A *dibe* lumbered in front of her, and she scrambled out of its way just in time. Desperately she looked around for Red, but he was gone. Suddenly she was knocked from behind and hooves stomped down all around her.

Lucky looked up, but the beasts filled the sky. *They scare me!* She wanted so much to bark. *But I can't. Grandpa will find me if I do.*

She scrambled to her feet, but didn't see the *dibe* almost on top of her. It knocked her down, and she crouched in the dust. Afraid to move, Lucky squeezed her eyes shut, her body trembling.

Then the image of Flint drifted through her mind. She imagined he sneered, "Look at her, she's scared. Worthless dog. I told you so."

Then she imagined Emerson shaking his head, his face full of disappointment. "I was wrong to bring you here, Lucky. You just don't have what it takes."

Shame flooded through her. *I'm lying here like a coward flat on my belly.* She began shaking with anger. *I'm the badger hunter, the **nahashch'id**. Those **dibe** should be scared of me!* She opened her eyes and stood up. *I'll show Flint. I'll show them all!*

Lucky turned and growled at the sheep plodding by. *You're just stupid **dibe**. I'm not afraid of you!* She puffed out her chest and arched her tail over her back. *I'm a **nahash ch'id**. Get out of my way, or you'll be sorry!*

She pushed forward, growling at any <u>dibe</u> that got too close. She discovered she could dodge around them and avoid their hooves. Lucky felt braver and braver with every step she took.

My boy should see me now! Emerson's face flashed before her eyes. *Oh no! I forgot him. He has to know I'm safe.* Lucky worked her way to the edge of the herd and saw him sitting on a huge horse. *I guess the horse isn't hurting him. He looks okay. I'll sneak out, so he can see me.*

Lucky crept to the edge of the herd and stood motionless, one paw in the air, staring at her boy. She saw him turn his head, searching for her. She risked a quick little bark to guide him. Emerson leaned quickly around in the saddle and looked right at her. *He sees me!* Lucky wagged her tail. *Uh-oh, Grandfather's turning around!* She darted back into the herd.

Suddenly Flint bounded right in front of her. "Red sent me to warn you. Don't leave the herd again, unless you want to go back to that trading post." Flint sneered, "I think you should go back. You won't make it out here. You're just a sissy dog."

The hairs on Lucky's back stood stiff. She arched her neck and stared into Flint's eyes. "I'm tough enough to be a sheepdog," she growled. "You'll see."

"Hmmph! Just do as you're told. It's a long walk to the grazing ground." He turned and loped back outside the herd.

Grrrr! Lucky's body shook with anger. *What an awful dog. I don't like him. He thinks he's so great and that I'm nothing. I'll show him he's wrong.*

Keeping up with the herd was difficult. The <u>dibe</u> took bigger steps, and Lucky sometimes had to run to stay in the center. Before long she started panting. It seemed like forever before the herd stopped and spread out to graze. Lucky spotted a bush big enough to shade her from the sun. Several ***dibe*** grazed next to it.

She crept underneath and stretched out in the cool dirt. *Ah, this feels good. If Emerson was here, we could take a nap together.*

Slowly the ***dibe*** moved to one side, and Lucky saw

her boy and his grandfather a distance away. She laid her muzzle on her front paws and watched, but she didn't move from her hiding place.

I hope Emerson gets away soon. She imagined playing with her boy and thumped her tail happily. *If I have to, I'll wait here all day,* she promised herself. *He'll think of something to get away from Grandpa. And when he does, I'll follow him.*

18
Riding Like a Cowboy

 Grandpa treats me like a baby. I hate that! Emerson's horse plodded next to his grandfather's. *He still won't let me hold the reins. Agghh!* Finally Emerson spoke up.

"Grandpa, I'm old enough to hold the reins myself. Besides, I watch cowboy movies on TV. I know what to do."

"**Shi Tsoi**, this is how I taught your mother. First she learned how her horse moved. Then she learned how to guide it."

"Yeah, but Mom was a girl, and I'm a boy. I can do this."

Grandpa Charlie didn't answer. He still held Emerson's reins, riding a little ahead.

I feel stupid hanging onto the saddle horn with two hands. I bet he'd never even notice if I let go. Emerson

119

slowly dropped one hand to dangle at his side. Then he rested the other one on top of the saddle horn. *I bet I look cool now. Just like a real cowboy.*

Suddenly a jackrabbit bolted under the pinto. The horse kicked its hind legs and Emerson pitched forward. His feet slid out of the stirrups and he began falling. Grandpa Charlie grabbed him by the shirt just in time.

His grandfather stopped the horses and helped Emerson back in the saddle. Sticking his feet through the stirrups, Emerson grabbed the saddle horn with both hands. His face flushed a deep red. "Thanks, Grandpa," Emerson's voice shook. "I'm okay. It looks a lot easier on TV."

"You learned a valuable lesson, **Shi Tsoi**. We are on level ground now. Are you ready to learn how to handle your horse?"

Emerson stayed quiet for a moment. He'd made a mistake in front of his grandfather. Now he needed Grandpa Charlie's help but didn't want to admit it. Finally he sighed and nodded his head. "I'm ready."

Grandpa Charlie showed Emerson how to make his horse stop by pulling back on the reins. He learned to go forward by squeezing the horse's sides with his legs. Then he practiced how to make his horse go faster and then slower.

At last the old man handed the reins to Emerson. "Are you ready to guide your horse by yourself?"

Emerson nodded, holding the reins like his grandfather had shown him.

"That's good." Grandpa Charlie smiled. "Do not move suddenly. When you want to stop, pull back steadily. Do not jerk the reins."

"Okay, Grandpa." He nudged the pinto with his heels. The horse moved forward, and Emerson passed his grandfather.

Wow! I'm riding all by myself! Man, would Zach be jealous. Emerson looked over his shoulder and grinned at his grandfather. Grandpa Charlie smiled back, but stayed a few paces behind.

Soon Emerson relaxed and stared at the mesa around him. *This place is pretty weird. Near the mountains it's pretty. But I'm glad I don't live here. No wonder Mom left.* He felt a pang in his heart and bit his lip. *I won't think about Mom now. I better think of a way to help Lucky.*

He checked the herd. He knew she was there somewhere. *When we stop, I'll make an excuse to get away. Then I'll find her.*

The sun had climbed in the sky before they reached the grazing grounds. He watched while Grandpa Charlie and the dogs herded the sheep to a stop. Emerson swiveled in his saddle, trying to find Lucky. *Her legs are so short. What if she couldn't keep up?* He saw the other dogs, but Lucky wasn't with them.

Grandpa Charlie dismounted and motioned for Emerson to do the same.

Emerson swung his leg over the saddle, but he couldn't reach the ground. Hanging on to the saddle horn, he slipped his other foot out of the stirrup and jumped to the ground. His knees buckled, and he almost fell.

Ow! My legs. My butt. Emerson leaned over and rubbed the sore parts. *Geez, I hope I can walk. I'll die if Grandpa sees me like this.* He gritted his teeth and took one step toward his grandfather's horse, then a second. The third step was definitely easier.

His grandfather's back was partially turned to him. He saw Grandpa Charlie cupping his hand over his mouth, coughing slightly. Emerson's eyebrows knit together. *Is he coughing? Or laughing? He laughed when Old Jack butted me.*

"Grandpa? He waited for his grandfather to turn around. "Maybe I should go count the ***dibe***. You know, make sure they're all here."

His grandfather nodded. "That's a good idea, ***Shi Tsoi***. After we tether the horses." When they were done, Grandpa Charlie opened his saddlebag. He pulled out a canteen, tin cup, a piece of jerky and an apple. Emerson shoved the apple and jerky into his pockets. Then he unbuckled his belt and looped the canteen and cup on it.

"Always stay where you can see the herd," his grandfather said. "The mesa looks flat, but it is not. There are many hills and arroyos. It's easy to get lost out here."

"I will, Grandpa," Emerson promised. He turned and walked toward the herd pretending to count the ***dibe***. He glanced over his shoulder. His grandfather was looking down at something in his hands.

Emerson walked through the herd looking left and right. Suddenly Lucky darted right in front of him jumping up and down. He dropped to his knees and scooped her up. "I thought I'd lost you!" He laughed out loud as she wiggled in his arms, licking his face.

He dropped his voice to a whisper and hunched over. "Did you know they almost took you away? How did you get loose? Did the other dogs help you?" He put her down and looked beyond the sheep. Grandpa was still looking down.

"We can't stay here, Lucky. See that arroyo? That means ditch to you. Let's run for it while grandpa's not looking. Ready?" Lucky wagged her tail.

"Okay, girl. Run!" Emerson turned to race toward the arroyo when Old Jack sprang out of the herd.

Emerson skidded to a stop, but Lucky shot past him toward the goat. She slowed down, but Old Jack ignored her. He eyed Emerson and pawed the ground.

"Oh, geez!" Then Old Jack lowered his head. Emerson lunged to one side and pushed a sheep between him and the goat. Old Jack sprang toward them.

"Get away from me!" Emerson hissed, hanging on to the sheep.

Old Jack and Emerson stared at each other and neither one moved. All of a sudden Lucky darted in front of the goat. She slid under his belly and bit his back leg. The goat bleated and whirled around, but Lucky jumped out of his way. Old Jack lowered his head and charged after her.

Emerson watched, helpless, while Lucky dodged between the *dibe*. Then he remembered that Old Jack never left the herd. If she ran away from the herd, they could both escape.

"Lucky! Come!" Emerson clapped his hands hard. He took off running, and she dashed after him. He looked behind him and saw Old Jack stop at the edge of the herd. Emerson didn't slow down. In seconds he and Lucky reached the arroyo and pitched forward down the bank.

19

Grandpa Surprises Me

 They tumbled to a stop at the bottom.

"We're safe, Lucky!" Emerson laughed and wrestled on the ground with his dog. Lucky snatched a stick in her teeth and shook it at him. He grabbed it from her mouth and threw it. Each time she brought it back, Emerson grabbed the stick and threw it again.

Hot and tired, they sat down to rest. "I bet you're thirsty, girl." Emerson poured water into his cup and shared it with his dog. He pulled out an apple and some jerky and bit off some bites for her. Lucky laid her muzzle on Emerson's knee while he talked to her.

"I don't understand Grandpa. He's my mom's dad, did you know that?"

Lucky thumped her tail.

"He was born here, on the reservation. When he

was little, his house didn't even have a bathroom. And he had to work hard, harder than Dad and Mom make me work." He patted Lucky's head.

"Grandpa wants to teach me things, like building fences and cooking fry bread. He says it's okay for us men to cook when we're at camp. Men have to take care of themselves."

Lucky climbed into Emerson's lap, and he hugged her. "Grandpa says men should always take care of people and animals. So I'll take care of you, Lucky. Always. I promise."

Emerson sighed. He had to tell his grandfather about Lucky. He squinted up at the sun and nudged his dog. "I've been gone awhile. Grandpa might start missing me. I'd better go back."

Just then Emerson heard his grandfather's voice. "Emerson! Where are you?"

He jumped up. "Don't move, Lucky," he whispered. "Let me talk to Grandpa first. Stay!" Lucky sat down.

Emerson climbed out of the arroyo and waved. "Here I am, Grandpa. I'm sorry. I forgot the time."

"The *dibe* are moving, and we must stay with them. Come back with me now."

"Grandpa, wait." Emerson took a few steps forward and stopped.

Grandpa Charlie hesitated a moment, then walked toward him. "What is it, *Shi Tsoi*?"

Emerson shoved his hands inside his pockets and

126

shuffled his weight back and forth. "I have to tell you something first."

His grandfather nodded.

Emerson's stomach churned. "Grandpa, I lied this morning. You asked where Lucky was, and I said I didn't know. That wasn't true." Emerson looked down at his feet as hot tears brimmed over his eyelashes. "Grandpa, Dad's gone off to war. He might get blown up, and I'll never see him again. Mom sent me to you 'cause I'm too much trouble." He wiped his wet cheeks with his sleeve. "I don't have any friends out here, Grandpa. Please let me keep her."

Grandpa Charlie knelt and gently tugged the glasses from Emerson's face. He wiped them dry on his bandana. "I know you did not tell me the truth," he said, placing the glasses back on Emerson's face. "I realized then how much the dog means to you. So I let her stay with the *dibe.*"

"WHAT?" Emerson's mouth dropped open. "You knew?"

His grandfather nodded.

"Why didn't you say something?"

"Because, *Shi Tsoi*, you had to tell me the truth first."

His grandfather's words hit him like a lightning bolt. Grandpa could have sent Lucky back, but he didn't! "Wait a minute. You're giving Lucky a second chance? You're letting me keep her?" His eyes searched deep into his grandfather's, but the old man looked away before speaking.

127

"First, let's see if it stays out of trouble." He stood up. "Now, call the dog. We must stay with the *dibe*."

Emerson's face broke into a delighted grin, and he clapped his hands together. "Lucky! Come here, girl!" She climbed out of the arroyo and ran to him. She scampered around his feet as they walked back to the horses.

I don't want to let her go. If she's going to be a sheepdog, she needs to be with them, not me. Emerson squatted and gave her a tiny shove toward the sheep. "It's okay, girl. Go help Red and Flint. I'll be right here on this horse. I won't leave you."

He watched Lucky race toward the herd. Then his grandfather boosted him up onto the pinto. *I get to keep Lucky! Woo-hoo!* Emerson rubbed his forehead. *Why'd Grandpa change his mind? He was so mean before.* He nudged his horse forward. *I don't get him. He's so different from Mom and Dad.*

He caught up with his grandfather. "Grandpa, can I ask you some questions?"

"Questions?" His grandfather's tone was not encouraging. "About what?"

"About you."

Grandpa Charlie shook his head slightly, then motioned with his hand. "Go ahead."

"Okay. There's a lot I don't understand. Like, why do you wait a long time before answering me?"

Grandpa Charlie looked surprised. "What do you mean?"

"Well, Grandpa, when I say something, you wait like a whole minute before you answer. Talking to you takes a really long time."

Grandpa Charlie answered slowly. "*Shi Tsoi*, I must be sure you have said all you wish to say before I speak. It is polite to wait. It is the Navajo way."

"Ooohhhhh." Emerson's voice trailed off as he tried to understand. His parents raised him to be polite, but they never told him about this.

They rode in silence for a few moments before Emerson said, "I have another question." He waited for Grandpa Charlie to nod before continuing. "How come you don't look at me when we talk? You look at my shoulder or the top of my head. And when I look at you, you look away. That feels really weird."

His grandfather sighed. "Your mother did not teach you respect?"

"Huh?" This puzzled Emerson. "What does that have to do with looking at me?"

"*Shi Tsoi*, polite Navajos do not look into another's eyes when they speak. This is rude, disrespectful. But many *Diné* live in the *bilagaana* world. They do not follow the old custom."

Now Emerson was really stumped. "No, Grandpa, it's supposed to show you're honest. How can it be rude?" He fidgeted in his saddle, waiting for his grandfather's answer. *This waiting business is really hard.*

Grandpa Charlie finally said, "It is the Navajo way.

We'll ask your mother to explain."

Emerson jumped, hearing several sharp screechy barks. *Lucky?* He twisted in his saddle and saw Old Jack charging in the middle of the herd. **Dibe** scattered in every direction. A tiny flash of brown dodged around them trying to escape from the goat.

"Lucky!" Emerson gasped, wheeling his horse around. "Old Jack's after Lucky!"

20

I Surprise Grandpa

 Emerson dug his heels into his horse, and the pinto bolted into a run. His butt slammed down on the saddle over and over. But he didn't care if it hurt. *I have to rescue my dog.*

Emerson headed the pinto right for Old Jack, but ***dibe*** ran in front of them. His horse swerved, and Emerson pulled hard on the reins. He managed to turn the horse around and spotted Lucky running through an open spot. Old Jack was gaining on her, his head lowered in a charge.

"Noooooo!" Emerson shouted. He wasn't going to make it in time!

Like a flash, Red darted through the ***dibe*** and slammed into Old Jack. The goat stumbled to one side, and Red rolled off onto the ground. Scrambling to his feet, Red faced Old Jack, his upper lip curled in a snarl.

133

Emerson jumped off his horse and grabbed Lucky just as the goat swung his head toward her. Red crouched and sprang closer to Old Jack, and the goat backed up. By crouching and springing, Red turned the goat and forced him back.

Emerson held Lucky out in front of him. "Are you all right, girl?" When she wiggled in his arms and licked his face, he knew she wasn't hurt. Emerson looked around for Old Jack, but he'd vanished into the herd. Then he saw Red loping back toward them.

Emerson put Lucky down and hugged the sheepdog. "Good dog! You saved Lucky!"

Red sniffed Lucky's head and body and licked her face. Then he turned and headed back to the herd.

Grandpa Charlie rode up and dismounted. "I see your dog is okay. The *dibe* look settled. We can rest for a while." He motioned for Emerson to sit in the shade of their horses.

Emerson settled Lucky on his lap and grinned at his grandfather. "Grandpa, let's talk. I've got lots more questions."

The old man held up his hand. "*Shi Tsoi*, you will be here all summer. There is plenty of time for talk."

Emerson thought about this for a moment. "You don't talk much, do you Grandpa?"

He shook his head. "No, *Shi Tsoi*. I talked to you more today than I talk to Sam in a month." The old man smiled. "Maybe two months."

"Hmmm. Me and my friends probably talk more than you. Mostly about homework and computer stuff and our soccer team. We watch soccer games on TV. Do you do that?"

His grandfather shook his head. "I do not have a television set."

"No television?" Emerson's jaw dropped open. "Why not?"

Grandpa Charlie shrugged. "It never seemed important."

"But if you get a TV, you can watch all sorts of good stuff." Emerson counted off on his fingers. "There's the History Channel with great stories about wars and the old wild west. And Nickelodeon has fun programs for kids. Mom and Dad watch it, too. And ESPN has sports like baseball and football and car racing. That's where we watch soccer."

Grandpa Charlie lifted an eyebrow, nodded once, but remained silent.

Emerson sighed. *Just as well we didn't stay at his house then. Wouldn't be any better there than out here.* The air was hot, even in the shade of their horses. Emerson yawned.

Grandpa Charlie glanced up at the sun. "This has been a long day for you. There are grazing grounds closer to camp. We'll head back."

Lucky scrambled to her feet when Emerson stood up. She took a few steps toward the sheep before looking back at her boy. Then she wagged her tail, turned, and took off after Red.

Emerson fought the urge to call her back. *I don't want her getting hurt. But she's staying close to Red now. He'll protect her.* Still, he felt a knot in his stomach.

His grandfather whistled to the dogs, then helped Emerson mount up. Slowly, they herded the *dibe* back toward camp.

Emerson hung back and watched his grandfather for a bit. *I can do that. If I stay behind the dibe, they'll go where I want.*

Nudging his horse forward, he fell in behind two lagging *dibe*. Emerson waved his hat and said "Hyah! Hyah!" The *dibe* began to move back to the herd.

Emerson laughed out loud. "I did it! They moved!" He looked around and spotted a few other stragglers near by. He rode up behind them and waved his hat. "Hyah! Hyah!" To his delight, this group moved toward the herd, too. *This isn't so hard. Just like cowboys on TV.*

Emerson saw his grandfather a short distance away and trotted over to join him. His butt didn't slam down on the saddle as much anymore. He was learning how to ride his horse, and he felt more like a cowboy. Soon his horse fell in step with his grandfather's.

"Grandpa, did you see me herding *dibe*?"

His grandfather smiled and nodded. "*Aoo*, I saw you. And I am proud."

Emerson's face flushed red. He looked down at his

saddle horn, feeling shy. "Grandpa, can I ask you one more question?"

His grandfather sighed deeply. "I fear this is going to be a very long summer for me." Then he nodded. "Ask your question."

"Okay. What's the Navajo word for grandfather?"

A big smile spread over Grandpa Charlie's face. "The words meaning 'my grandfather' are *Shi Cheii.* Can you say that?"

"*Shi Cheii,*" Emerson repeated slowly. *I'll say it over and over so I don't forget.*

He grinned and reined his horse around. "I'll ride near the back of the herd, Gra— I mean, *Shi Cheii.*" Emerson realized he felt more confident and happier, too, all of a sudden. *I haven't been happy since Dad left. I miss him. He'd be proud of me.* Thinking of his father made his throat hurt and his eyes water. He pushed those thoughts away.

Looking around for Lucky, Emerson saw her tagging after Red. He guided his horse so he could ride closer to her. *I bet Red's showing her how to be a sheepdog.* He watched her for a while. *I'm so proud of her. The best part of coming here is I found Lucky. And Shi Cheii says I can keep her. Well, so long as she stays out of trouble.*

Emerson frowned at first. Then he shrugged. Lucky was being good now and he felt way too happy to think about anything else. *She'll do okay,* he said to himself.

Besides, what could possibly go wrong now?

21
They Can't Have Her

A whole week's gone by, and Lucky's been a good dog. Emerson grinned, watching her follow Red through the sheep herd. *It's a miracle!* Then he shook his head. *No, it's a miracle **Shi Cheii** didn't catch her.*

Two times Emerson found Lucky inside the footlocker scratching at flour and sugar sacks. But he got her out before his grandfather noticed. *It's my own fault for tuning my back on her. Sheesh! But mostly she's learning to be a sheepdog.*

Emerson still thought about his friends back home, but now he didn't miss them so much. He and Lucky had jobs during the day, but they played together while the *dibe* grazed, and she sat with him while he ate lunch. At night she watched him help with dinner, following him back and forth from the footlocker to the campfire.

Last night he peered into the darkness after dinner and realized he didn't care where he was. *Sure it'd be great to be doing things with Zach. But here is okay, too. Lucky and me, we're learning stuff we'd never learn back home. She's like me. Maybe that's why I found her.*

The next day was a long one. Emerson and Grandpa Charlie rode the horses to the grazing ground. The sun shone lower on the horizon when they rode over the hill overlooking sheep camp.

"Look, **Shi Cheii.**" Emerson pointed to the **bighans.** "They're open. And there's Sam's truck. What's he doing here?"

They followed the **dibe** and dogs down the hill to the edge of camp. Lucky rode on the saddle in front of Emerson, her front legs hanging over one side and her back legs over the other. He'd picked her up earlier when she began lagging behind.

"**Ya'at'eeh,** Sam," Grandpa Charlie dismounted, letting Red and Flint round up the flock. "Why are you here?"

"This morning I stopped at the trading post in Bobcat Ridge." Sam glanced over at Emerson sitting on top of the pinto. He lowered his voice and began speaking to Grandpa Charlie in Navajo.

Emerson saw his grandfather dart a quick glance at him, then turn back to Sam.

"Gee, Lucky, I wonder what they're saying?" He concentrated on hearing the new sounds. "Something about a *kin* — that's a store," he said to his dog. "And there's that word for dog that I can't pronounce." He felt uneasy all of a sudden. "Are they talking about you?" He wished Grandpa would take Lucky so he could get off his horse.

Emerson watched his grandfather shake his head and walk toward him. Sam turned to the *dibe bighans* and pushed a few slowpoke *dibe* inside.

Grandpa Charlie reached for Lucky and held her. Emerson swung his leg over his horse and jumped to the ground. Taking Lucky from his grandfather, Emerson said, "Is something wrong, *Shi Cheii?*"

"*Aoo, Shi Tsoi.* Sam brings bad news for you." His grandfather looked past Emerson's head to the mesa behind him. "The dog's owner called Jolene, asking if she'd found it. They want it back."

Emerson's stomach lurched. He blinked his eyes, trying to breathe. "What?" His voice squeaked. His knees felt wobbly. "No, Grandpa. No."

Grandpa Charlie knelt beside Emerson. "Sometime after we left the trading post with the dog, its owner called. Jolene told the truth, that their dog was safe with us. They want to come get her. Jolene called my cell phone, but service out here…" He shrugged. "When Sam stopped at Bobcat Ridge this morning, Jolene asked him to bring me the message."

Emerson barely heard his grandfather's words. *This isn't happening. It's all wrong.* He hugged Lucky to his chest.

"I am sorry, **Shi Tsoi.** Sam says when he agreed, Jolene called the owner. They want to pick her up Saturday at the trading post."

Emerson shook his head hard. "No! They can't have her, **Shi Cheii.** Lucky doesn't love them. She loves me."

"**Shi Tsoi,** we are **Diné.** We do not keep property belonging to someone else. We'll find you another dog."

"I don't want another dog!" Emerson spat his words. "Lucky's mine, and I'm going to keep her. You can't make me give her back."

His grandfather stood. "Yes, Emerson, I can," he said in a low voice. "Today is Thursday. We leave for the trading post Saturday morning." He turned and walked toward the **dibe bighans.**

Lucky wiggled to be let down, but Emerson held her close. "I thought he'd changed, Lucky, but I was wrong. He was just pretending to be nice. A real grandpa would let me keep you."

Emerson's throat ached, and he couldn't talk anymore. He hugged Lucky and whispered, "I'll never let you go. Never."

"Emerson," Grandpa Charlie called.

Emerson looked over his shoulder. "I bet he expects me to go help. Why should I? He won't help me." Emerson looked out over the mesa. *I know how to reach the highway. We could leave now, but soon it'll be dark. Coyotes hunt at night. They might attack us.* He looked down at his dog in horror. *They might eat Lucky!*

"Emerson," Grandpa Charlie started walking toward him.

"Oh cripes, he's coming. Okay, girl, we'll get out of here tomorrow. I'll think of something."

He set Lucky on the ground and faced his grandfather. "You should be on my side, *Shi Cheii,* not theirs."

Grandpa Charlie folded his arms across his chest. "*Shi Tsoi,* she belongs to another family. If you kept the dog, you would be stealing. We are *Diné.* We do not steal."

"But she's mine, Grandpa. I'm not stealing her." His voice shook, but he was not going to give in. "Just because Mom's Navajo or *Diné* or whatever, you think I should do what you do."

Grandpa Charlie was quiet for a moment. "I'm sorry, *Shi Tsoi.* There is no other way. Perhaps when they see you and Lucky together, they may not want the dog back." He turned and motioned for Emerson to follow. "Come now and help with dinner."

Emerson knelt to pet Lucky. She climbed into his lap and licked his hand. He looked into her big brown eyes. "Not want you back? Not a chance." He scooped her up and followed his grandfather. *I'll show him. This time, I'll do what I want.*

The next morning, Emerson woke to the smell of wet dirt in the air. He dressed quickly and coaxed Lucky out of the warm sleeping bag. "You have to stay with me all day, girl. When I see a chance to sneak away, I won't have time to come look for you."

Emerson sat down on the log in front of the campfire. Lucky scampered over to Flint and Red.

Grandpa Charlie handed Emerson his breakfast and cup of coffee. "There was heavy rain north of us last night." He pointed to large dark clouds overhead. "You should leave the dog in camp today. Clouds are gathering; it will rain here."

Emerson shook his head. "No, Grandpa. This is our last day together. I want her with me." He stared at his plate and took a bite of beans and onions. He did not look at his grandfather.

22
Danger!

 Emerson slammed both footlockers shut and covered the dogs' food bin. Then he helped his grandfather lug them to the sleeping shelter. He rolled up the sleeping bags while Grandpa Charlie unfolded some plastic tarps.

"Put the sleeping bags and clothes on top of the footlockers," Grandpa Charlie said. Once this was done, he spread the tarps over everything and tied them together with a rope.

"It will rain soon," Grandpa Charlie said. "How hard, I do not know. We'll take the *dibe* to graze not far from here." He looked down at Lucky. "You should tie the dog to the footlocker."

Emerson shook his head. "No. What if she gets scared, and I'm not here? I'll tie her to my belt. That way she won't wander off. If it rains hard, I'll carry her."

Grandpa Charlie shook his head and sighed. Then he turned toward the **bighans**.

They herded the **dibe** in a new direction but had to walk a long way around a big arroyo. Soon, Grandpa Charlie whistled to the dogs to stop. Lucky began pulling on her rope. *She probably has to go pee,* he thought and let her loose. "Come right back," he told her.

The wind came up, and the smell of rain was everywhere. Huge dark clouds covered the sky. *They look like giants ready to fight,* Emerson thought.

Gritting his teeth, he wondered if the rain would help his plan. *I paid attention. I know how to get back to camp. We'll take a short cut. We'll climb down that arroyo and up the other side. Grandpa will never see us.*

It seemed like no time at all before raindrops began stinging his face. He pulled his huge hat down to block them. Now he was glad he wore Grandpa's over-sized hat.

Grandpa Charlie appeared at his side. "We will move the **dibe** slowly back to camp so they can graze while they walk. Where's your dog?"

Emerson looked around, but didn't see her. "I bet she's with Red. I'll find her and tie her to me." He felt guilty for letting her out of his sight. Grandpa Charlie began moving the herd while Emerson zigzagged through the **dibe**.

Finally he spotted Lucky trailing along the edge of the herd. He could barely see her through the rain. The sheepdogs were busy rounding up stragglers and paid no attention to her.

A loud clap of thunder filled the air, and he jumped. When he looked back for Lucky, she was gone. Emerson ran through the *dibe*, looking for her. Circling his mouth with his hands, he yelled, "Lucky! Lucky!"

A sharp bark pierced through the rain, and he turned toward it. Off in a distance, he saw her, standing all alone. Thunder roared again, and lightning split the sky. Lucky turned and bolted away.

"No! Come back!" Emerson sprinted after her, wiping rain from his glasses as he ran. "Where'd she go?" He slowed and looked around. "There she is. Lucky! Here, girl!"

It seemed she didn't hear him. Another crash of thunder and lightning startled her, and she bolted again. *She's scared! I have to catch her.* Then she disappeared right in front of his eyes. He slowed down and realized he was running along the edge of the arroyo. He stopped and looked down. *There she is, at the bottom.*

Emerson started walking down the side but slipped and landed on his butt. He pushed himself up and half slid the rest of the way down. Scrambling to his feet, he ran to Lucky and picked her up.

"Poor little Lucky." She shivered next to his chest. "You look like a drowned rat. Don't be scared, I'm here. I'll take care of you."

He realized his grandfather didn't know where he

was. Emerson looked down at his shivering dog. "This is it, Lucky! We can escape. Grandpa can't see us down here." He started walking. "We have to get as close to camp as possible. I think I remember where we climb up to the other side. We'll beat Grandpa back to camp and grab some food. I bet someone driving along the highway will pick us up."

Excitement raced through him. He was really going to do it! They would make it back to Bobcat Ridge, and he'd call Mom – but not from the trading post. They'd go to the gas station, where no one would recognize him or Lucky.

He kept walking and looking for the place to climb up. Lucky squirmed in his arms, so he tightened his grip. Then she began barking. Barking at HIM. Faintly he heard a strange sort of rumbling sound. *Huh. Wonder what that is?*

"What's wrong, girl?" The moment he stopped, Lucky pushed herself out of his arms and leapt to the ground. She jumped up and barked at him. When he reached for her, she darted away toward the bank. Then she barked again and scrambled up a little way.

The rumbling noise seemed a little louder now. "What is it? Lucky, stop barking! You're going up the wrong side! Come here!"

But she didn't move. "Oh, man." He trudged toward her. When he reached for her, she scrambled farther up the bank. "Stop it, Lucky. You're making me mad." He

148

started climbing after her and she backed up even farther. "We have to go up the OTHER side," he yelled.

She turned to look at the bank behind her, and Emerson lunged for her. "Aha! Gotcha!" But she snarled and bit into his sleeve. Shocked, Emerson dropped her. Lucky jumped to her feet, snagged his sleeve again and yanked hard with her teeth.

It's like she wants me to follow her. He pulled his arm away. Lucky turned and scrambled to the top. Just then, Emerson realized the rumbling noise sounded much closer now. Something about it just wasn't right. He looked up, but Lucky was gone. His heart began pounding in his chest.

"Don't run, Lucky. I'm coming." He started crawling up the steep bank, but the wet dirt was slippery. Suddenly, a rock fell out from under his feet. He slid all the way back down.

He got to his knees and began clawing his way up again. He could see a bush a little way up. I can grab onto that, he thought. He buried his fingers into the dirt and pushed up with his toes. The noise was so close now he could feel it inside his head.

Rain splattered his glasses and he couldn't see the bush. He paused to wipe them with his sleeve. *I see it! I'm almost there!* The rumbling now sounded like a freight train pounding in his ears. He peered through the rain to the far end of the arroyo and saw…water? No! A wall of water! Barreling through the arroyo, heading straight for him.

Emerson screamed and clawed the wet dirt with his hands. Pushing hard with his feet, he flung his arm up and gripped the bush. Suddenly water swirled around his feet, and they shot out from under him. He clung to the bush with all his strength.

"Help!" he yelled. "Help me!"

23
Now What?

"Shi Tsoi! I'm here." Grandpa Charlie's voice boomed over the flood and the rain.

A foot thudded next to Emerson's head, and a hand gripped his shoulder. "Grab my arm!" his grandfather shouted.

Emerson let go of the bush and clawed the air above him. He couldn't see through his foggy glasses. Then his hands hit something — Grandpa Charlie's knee — and he clung to it. He felt his grandfather's hands under his armpits. With a firm grip, Grandpa Charlie lifted him up.

Emerson gagged from rain sliding down his throat and up his nose. But he wouldn't let go of the knee. He felt Grandpa Charlie side step up the bank, dragging Emerson with him. It seemed like forever before his grandfather heaved them both over the edge of the bank.

"Shi Cheii," Emerson pulled himself to his grand-

father's chest and held tight. "*Shi Cheii,* you saved me! I — I — I…" Suddenly he jerked away. "Lucky!" he shouted. "Where's Lucky?"

A little brown streak jumped on Grandpa Charlie's lap and landed in Emerson's arms.

"You're safe!" Emerson half laughed, half cried while she wiggled in his arms, licking his face. All at once his arms and legs went limp, and he couldn't hold up his head. "*Shi Cheii,* I don't feel good. I better lie down." He curled up on the ground with his dog.

Grandpa Charlie got up on one knee and lifted Emerson to a sitting position. "I will carry you back to camp." He hoisted Emerson over one shoulder and stood. "Your dog must follow behind."

Emerson lay like a sack of potatoes tossed over his grandfather's shoulder. He'd never felt so weak before. He opened his eyes now and then to be sure Lucky was still behind them. Before long, the wind died down, and the rain only drizzled. Emerson felt strength return to his arms and legs. When he felt strong enough, he said, "*Shi Cheii,* I bet I can walk now."

His grandfather lowered him to the ground. At first his legs trembled a bit. Lucky jumped around his feet, and he felt strong enough to pick her up. He looked up at Grandpa Charlie. He knew he had to say something.

"You saved me, *Shi Cheii.* I — I…"

"Shhh. We will talk later." He ruffled his grandson's hair. "You lost your hat."

Emerson smiled. "Guess now I'll get a new one, huh?"

Emerson pushed one foot in front of the other, determined to walk back to camp. When they finally reached the **bighans**, Grandpa Charlie turned Emerson toward the sleeping shelter.

"Go put on dry clothes and lie down. The dogs and I will handle the **dibe**." He shook his head at Lucky, dripping water. "Dry your dog, or you will have a wet sleeping bag."

Emerson headed for the sleeping shelter and stripped off his wet clothes. Quickly he pulled on warm dry ones and unrolled his sleeping bag. Then he rubbed Lucky with a towel and wrapped her in his last clean shirt. Just seconds after burrowing inside the sleeping bag, he fell asleep.

When Emerson woke, the rain had stopped. He smelled coffee and ham cooking, and his stomach rumbled. "Wake up, Lucky. Grandpa's got food!"

They rolled out of the sleeping bag and hurried to the campfire. Emerson noticed a small bowl of dog food next to the log. So did Lucky. She wolfed down her dinner in a few bites.

Grandpa Charlie handed Emerson a plate of ham, chile, and potatoes. "Let's eat in the sleeping shelter, **Shi Tsoi.** It's too wet to sit here." Then he poured Emerson a cup of coffee and stirred in a packet of instant cocoa.

Soon they sat cross-legged on Emerson's sleeping

bag. His grandfather said nothing during the meal. Emerson finished first, cleaned off his plate, and put it in the footlocker. He walked back to his grandfather and asked, "Want more coffee, **Shi Cheii?** I'll get it."

Grandpa Charlie nodded and handed Emerson his cup. He poured the last of the coffee while his grandfather cleaned off his plate. Then they sat down together on the sleeping bag.

Emerson took a deep breath. "I still can't believe I could have died. I was so scared, and suddenly you were there. You saved my life." He looked up at his grandfather. "I can say thank you all day long, but it wouldn't be good enough. So much stuff's mixed up inside me. But I don't know how to say it."

"Begin by telling me what happened, **Shi Tsoi.**"

Emerson hung his head. *What do I tell Grandpa? That I was running away? He saved my life.* He glanced at his grandfather but quickly looked down again.

"Emerson," his grandfather said, "your face tells me you wish to hide something." He sipped his coffee. "You should tell me the truth."

Emerson looked down at Lucky, curled up in his lap. This wasn't going to be easy.

"**Shi Cheii,** Lucky and me, we were running away. That's why we were in the arroyo. I thought if I crossed up the other side close to camp, you wouldn't see us. Then we'd grab some food and walk to the highway."

"You did not see the danger in your plan?" His

grandfather frowned.

Emerson shook his head. "I didn't think of the plan till I caught Lucky at the bottom."

"So you followed the dog into the arroyo?" Grandpa Charlie's voice sounded angry.

Immediately, Emerson realized his mistake. "No, **Shi Cheii.** It wasn't like that. She was scared of the thunder and lightning, and she didn't know where she was going, so I went down to get her. That's when I planned our escape."

"Did I not tell you to leave the dog in camp?"

Emerson remained silent for a moment, then nodded. "But I already decided last night to run away when you weren't looking. That's why I took her with me."

"Such foolishness, **Shi Tsoi.**" Grandpa Charlie shook his head. "Because of that dog, you could have drowned. You know that, don't you?"

Tears welled up in Emerson's eyes. He did know that. He still felt the cold swirling water pulling his feet, and terror gripped his heart all over again. "But you saved me, **Shi Cheii.** Just in time. How did you find me?"

Grandpa Charlie took a big swig of coffee before answering. "When you didn't come back with your dog, I started looking for you. I called your name, but you did not answer." He was silent for a moment.

"Then I heard water flooding down the arroyo. I ran to the edge, but couldn't see you. Suddenly your dog ran up to me, barking. You are always together, so I knew something was wrong. The dog turned and ran along the edge of the bank. I followed behind, and when the dog stopped, I saw you. I climbed down and grabbed your shoulder. You know the rest."

Emerson pulled Lucky to his chest and held her tight. "So that's why I didn't see you. You went to get help." He wiped tears from his face and nose with his sleeve. "*Shi Cheii,* Lucky helped you save me. You can't give her back to those other people."

Grandpa Charlie looked down at Emerson. "You know I don't approve of this dog. It is useless out here. Today you tried to run away with it, and look what happened."

"And I'll try again, Grandpa. As soon as you're asleep."

"Another bad idea, *Shi Tsoi. Ma'ii* hunt at night. They will attack you and your dog."

"Then I'll wait till sun-up. I won't stay here without Lucky."

Grandpa Charlie looked out over the mesa. "Sam will be here tomorrow morning. Then we'll take the dog to the trading post."

Emerson gasped. "No, *Shi Cheii!* No."

His grandfather stood. "Why is this dog so important to you?"

How can I make him understand? I don't even understand. The words came out slowly. "It's like I'm, well, lost. Kind of. When I was really little, I had a bad

156

dream. I was trapped someplace dark, where I didn't belong, and I couldn't get out." He looked up at his grandfather. "That's what it's like now. I don't belong out here. Lucky doesn't either. But we're here together, and I don't feel trapped anymore. She's supposed to be my dog." He wiped his nose with his sleeve. "I can't tell you why. I just KNOW."

His grandfather waited longer than usual to answer. "It is a mystery. Because of the dog, you almost died." He looked out over the mesa. "Yet, because of the dog, you lived."

"That's what I'm trying to tell you, *Shi Cheii.*"

Grandpa Charlie gazed at Emerson and Lucky for quite a while. Then he sighed and reached for his sleeping bag. "I will think about what you said, *Shi Tsoi.* We will see what happens tomorrow. Perhaps those people will change their minds."

"*Shi Cheii,* that's not — "

Grandpa Charlie held up his hand. "Emerson, enough. I said I will think about what you told me." He turned his back and rolled out his sleeping bag.

24
Don't Make Me Do This

"*Shi Tsoi,* wake up." Grandpa Charlie shook Emerson's shoulder.

Emerson opened his eyes enough to see his grandfather kneeling beside him. When he tried to sit up, his forehead throbbed. "My head hurts, *Shi Cheii.*" He sank back down.

"I bet more than your head hurts, *Shi Tsoi.* Come eat. You will feel better."

Slowly Emerson rolled over and watched his grandfather walk back to the campfire. Lucky burrowed out from the sleeping bag and pounced on his chest.

"No, Lucky," he groaned, forcing himself to sit up. "Everything hurts. My head, my shoulders, my arms… even my fingers. It's worse than the first week of soccer practice."

Emerson scooted Lucky to the ground. Slowly, he

crawled out of his sleeping bag and dressed. "Mmmphhh," he groaned again, pushing himself up. Only the aroma from his grandfather's skillet kept him moving. He sat on the log, and Grandpa Charlie handed him a bean burrito.

"Take this, too," his grandfather handed Emerson a mug. "Coffee with cocoa. It will help your headache. When you are done eating, I have something else for you."

Lucky wolfed down her breakfast and raced over to the other dogs. Like in a dream, Emerson chewed his breakfast burrito and sipped his coffee. *My head hurts so much, I can't think, and today I lose Lucky. I want this all to be a bad dream. I want to go back to sleep and wake up again, and everything will be all right.*

When they finished eating, Grandpa Charlie handed Emerson a small leaf. "This is feverfew. It will help your headache and sore muscles. Chew it well before you swallow it."

Emerson stared at the leaf. *Chew this? Mom gives me aspirin.* He bit into it and chewed. "Yuck! This tastes bad!" He started to spit it out, but Grandpa Charlie put his hand over Emerson's mouth.

"*Shi Tsoi,* chew it and swallow it." His grandfather's voice was stern.

Emerson did as he was told, hating every moment. He forced it down his throat and took a big gulp of his now cool coffee.

Grandpa Charlie smiled. "You will feel better soon. Go lie down and rest. Sam is not here yet."

Emerson called Lucky to him, and they walked to his sleeping bag. She curled up next to him while he took off his boots and his glasses. He placed his glasses on the toe of his boot, then closed his eyes and drifted off. He woke suddenly with Lucky licking his face.

Sitting up, he rubbed his forehead and looked around. Grandpa Charlie and Sam stood at the **bighans**, talking. Emerson rolled over onto his knees. His head didn't throb so much now, and his muscles didn't feel as sore, either. Slowly he stood and walked to his grandfather. Lucky ran off to join the sheepdogs.

Sam smiled at him. "I am glad to see you alive, boy." Then he added, "I am sorry about your dog."

Emerson looked up at his grandfather, who glanced away. "Get the dog, **Shi Tsoi.** We need to go."

Emerson stared down at his boots. He couldn't move. A lump rose in his throat, but he couldn't even cry. "I can't," was all he could say.

Grandpa Charlie waited for a moment, then turned and walked to Lucky. He picked her up and tucked her under his arm. "Come, Emerson. Or stay here with Sam. You choose."

Emerson looked up and slowly reached for his dog. "I'll take her," he whispered. He held Lucky tight to his chest while he got in the truck and shut the door.

They rode in silence. Emerson stared out the window. *I remember this feeling. The morning Dad left. I sat in the back seat and couldn't move. He was going away, and I couldn't stop him. I couldn't even say good-bye.*

He looked down at Lucky. *I can't just give up. I have to fight for her.* He looked over at his grandfather, feeling his stomach twist into knots. Words came tumbling out.

"**Shi Cheii,** don't give her back. I'll do anything. Anything you say. I'll work hard. I'll never disobey you again. I'll learn Navajo. I'll make you breakfast. I'll shovel poop from the **dibe bighans** all by myself. You won't even have to help me."

Grandpa Charlie looked over at Emerson and sighed. Then he lifted one hand from the steering wheel and brushed Emerson's hair up off his forehead. He glanced quickly at the road and then back at his grandson.

"I have a good feeling about today, **Shi Tsoi.**" He placed his hand back on the steering wheel and looked straight ahead.

Emerson's jaw dropped open. *Good feeling? He has a good feeling? What does that mean? Does he know something I don't?* Thoughts tumbled around inside his mind until they reached Bobcat Ridge. By then his gloomy thoughts were fading away. *Maybe those people won't even show up. Grandpa says he has a good feeling.*

Emerson saw the trading post up ahead with a big SUV parked out front. His heart sank. He just knew it was them. "They're already here, **Shi Cheii.**"

Grandpa Charlie pulled in and parked. Then he honked. This time Emerson was in no hurry to leave the truck. Besides, someone was on the porch, smoking a cigarette. A woman.

Grandpa Charlie reached over and opened Emerson's door. He slid off the seat with Lucky in his arms and walked to the hood. Grandpa Charlie put a hand on Emerson's shoulder and guided him toward the porch.

The woman watched them walk up. She flicked the cigarette butt on the porch and stubbed it out. She was not very tall, with short black hair. Emerson climbed the steps and looked into her eyes. They were so dark they looked black. First she stared at him. Then she stared at Lucky. She ignored Grandpa Charlie.

The woman leaned forward and frowned. "I'm Rhonda Serna. Harold and the children are inside. Let's get this over with."

Emerson's hope vanished.

25

I Won't Leave My Boy

(Lucky)

Lucky sniffed at the woman. *What's she doing here? I hope those bratty kids aren't with her.* Lucky squirmed in Emerson's arms and looked up. His face looked scrunched up and sad. She looked at Grandpa Charlie. His face looked grim.

Mrs. Serna turned her back, her purse swinging from her shoulder. She walked through the door. She did not hold it open for Emerson or Grandpa Charlie.

The moment they walked inside, Lucky spotted the kids. *Oh no! It's them.* Lucky clutched Emerson's wrist with her front paws and whined.

"There's the dog! Give it to me!" A boy ran up and reached for Lucky.

She shrank back against Emerson's chest.

"Give IT to you?" Emerson backed away, dumb-struck. "Didn't you give her a name?

"Nah, we didn't have her long enough." The boy jerked Lucky from Emerson's arms. Her legs paddled the air like a windmill. *Save me, Emerson,* she yelped.

"Noooooo! Give her to ME! I want to hold her." The girl ran over and pulled Lucky's leg, trying to pry her from her brother's hands.

Ouch! Lucky struggled to get away from both of them. *Leave me alone.*

Emerson jerked the girl's shoulder. "Stop it! You're hurting my dog."

"Yeah, let go of it," the boy sneered. "I'm older. I get first dibs." He yanked Lucky away from his sister and held her in the air.

Help me! Lucky yelped for her boy and struggled to get to him. Emerson reached for her, but the boy jerked her back. "Don't touch her. She's not yours."

I hate these kids. I hate them! Lucky barked and scratched the boy's arm.

"Daaaad," the girl cried. "Bentley's being mean to me."

"Take it easy, kids," Mr. Serna said. "Bentley, give Clarissa the dog. Now."

No, don't do it! She's even worse than you. Lucky twisted around and tried to crawl over Bentley's shoulder.

"Stop that!" Bentley pulled Lucky from his shoulder and thrust her at Clarissa. Lucky struggled so hard she slipped from Clarissa's hands. She hit the floor with a thud.

I'm free! Lucky jumped to her feet, but her back leg hurt. Suddenly she saw hands everywhere reaching down for her. Quickly she spun around and skittered away on three feet. Bentley and Clarissa chased right behind her, pushing each other to be first.

Emerson followed at their heels. "Leave Lucky alone! I mean it."

Lucky skidded around a corner and stopped. Blankets and rugs were piled everywhere on the floor. *Where can I hide?*

"Not the rug room!" She heard Jolene yell. "Get out of the rug room!"

Lucky dove under a small pile of blankets and wiggled to the center. *They'll never find me here.*

She heard the brats stomp into the room, arguing, followed by sounds of things being moved. "She's in here, we'll get her," Bentley said.

"I said get out of the rug room!" Jolene's voice was loud and sharp. "Now!" Lucky heard Jolene's footsteps coming closer to her hiding place. "The rugs could be damaged." It sounded like she was picking up scattered rugs.

"There she is," Bentley shouted. "Her tail's sticking out."

Dang it! I forgot to hide my tail. Lucky tried to crawl out the other side, but she was too late. The rug covering her lifted up, and Clarissa gasped. "Grab her!"

Lucky bolted for the door, but Bentley's legs blocked the way.

"Aha. Gotcha!" Bentley reached down, but Clarissa rammed him with her shoulder. He staggered to the side.

"No, I got her," she bent down for Lucky.

"No, you don't!" Bentley pushed her away.

Lucky darted between their legs, barely escaping their hands. *Emerson,* she barked. *Help me!* She scampered down a short aisle, her heart pounding in her chest. Skidding around the corner, another pair of feet stood in front of her. *It's my boy!*

"Lucky, stop!" Emerson dove and picked her up before Bentley grabbed her again. He turned and ran to the counter where Jolene stood. She bent over and put her arm around Emerson's shoulder.

"This is my store," she almost shouted. "Stop this now!"

"I want the dog, Daaaad!" Clarissa started crying.

"Make him give it to me, Dad." Bentley shook his fist at Emerson.

"Now, kids…" Mr. Serna tried to soothe the situation, but they wouldn't shut up.

Horrible brats! They hurt my ears. Lucky twisted in Emerson's arms and started barking at them. *I'll never go back with you. I ran away before, and I'll run away again.*

"Lucky's mine!" Emerson shouted. "No one gets her."

"It's not your dog!" Bentley shouted back. "Give it to me."

Clarissa started crying again. "No! To ME." She tugged at her father's shirt.

Suddenly, Bentley lunged at Emerson and grabbed Lucky by the neck. He started to pull, and Lucky yelped.

"Stop hurting her!" Emerson yelled. He let go of Lucky with one hand and socked Bentley with his fist. But Emerson lost his balance when Bentley dropped to his knees. Lucky tumbled to the floor.

Before anyone could move, she scooted around Bentley's legs to the cash register counter. *I see a place to hide, if I can just get there.*

"Catch her! Catch her!" Clarissa squealed, chasing after her.

Lucky skidded to a stop and squeezed under the counter just in time. *I'm safe! And I won't come out until they leave.*

Lucky watched Clarissa and Bentley's hands poke around under the counter. Clarissa stretched her arm and caught the end of Lucky's tail. "I got her!"

No, you don't. Lucky twisted around and bit the girl's hand.

"Owww!" Clarissa let go, pulling back her hand. "Bad dog! She bit me! Daaad, get her out and spank her."

The kids kept shouting, and Emerson kept yelling for them to shut up. Lucky started barking. *If they think I'm a really bad dog, maybe they'll go away.*

Suddenly, a loud boom thundered through the room. Lucky jumped, her little heart hammering in her chest. *What was that?*

26
It's a Miracle

 Emerson almost jumped out of his skin. He spun around just as Grandpa Charlie slammed his fist on the counter a second time.

"Be quiet! All of you!" Grandpa Charlie roared. "I will buy the dog."

The store fell silent.

Emerson couldn't believe his ears. "What, *Shi Cheii?*"

"I will buy the dog," Grandpa Charlie repeated, opening his wallet.

"No! It's our dog! We get it!" Bentley and Clarissa cried.

While they argued, Emerson knelt down and put his hand under the counter. "Poor little Lucky. Come here. I won't let them take you. I promise." Slowly she crawled out and crept into his arms. He stood up.

171

"We're not selling," Mr. Serna began. "We came all this way, and the children — "

"Harold!" The black-eyed woman snapped. "Do what the man says. Be quiet." Emerson's jaw dropped. In all the noise, he'd forgotten about Grandpa Charlie and Mrs. Serna. She leaned against the counter next to his grandfather.

"You want to buy the dog?" She turned to Grandpa Charlie and tapped the counter with red, manicured nails. "How much?"

Grandpa Charlie pulled money from his wallet. "I have thirty dollars."

"No way!" Mr. Serna protested. "I paid a whole lot more than thirty dollars for that dog, plus all her shots."

"Yeah, no way!" Bentley sneered. "You lose."

"Bentley!" Mrs. Serna jabbed her finger at her son. "You be quiet, too. I'm handling this now." She walked over to her husband.

"Harold, I've wasted an entire morning already. I have a ticket to the symphony this afternoon. If I miss it, I'll not be happy. You know how I love Vivaldi."

She turned to her children. "Bentley. Clarissa. Don't move. Don't talk."

Mrs. Serna walked over to Emerson and looked into his eyes. "Young man, give me the dog. I want to see her." She held out her hands.

Swallowing hard, Emerson lifted Lucky so Mrs. Serna could hold her. His throat choked up as he let go.

"Please, lady…"

Mrs. Serna stepped back, holding Lucky at arm's length in front of her. They stared into each other's eyes for a few moments. Then her lips curved into a small smile, and she nestled Lucky in her arms.

"You are a sweet little dog, aren't you?" she whispered, placing a small kiss on Lucky's nose. Lucky looked up at her and wagged her tail.

Mrs. Serna straightened her back and looked hard at her children. "Owning a dog is a big responsibility," she said. "I wonder if you children know what that means."

"It means I have to play with her. But I won't clean up her poop," Bentley said. "That's nasty!"

"Me neither," Clarissa shook her head.

"Uh huh. Just what I thought." Mrs. Serna turned to Emerson. "Why should I give this dog to you?"

"Because, because … we belong together." Emerson's mouth felt so dry he could barely get the words out.

"That's not what I asked." She pointed her finger at him. "Can you handle responsibility, young man? Will you take care of this dog? Feed her? Protect her?"

Suddenly, Emerson felt a glimmer of hope. He nodded eagerly. "Yes ma'am. She'll get her meals on time because I'll feed her myself. She sleeps with me, too. I watch her all day long. When I get home, I'll walk her on a leash so she doesn't get hurt. And I'll clean up her poop, Mrs. Serna, every day. I'll do anything to keep Lucky." He took a small step forward. "Me and Lucky, we're best friends."

A big, warm smile spread across Mrs. Serna's face, and Emerson could see her eyes sparkle. "Then I believe this little dog belongs to you." She handed Lucky back to Emerson.

"Woo-hoo! Lucky! I can keep you!!" Emerson hugged his dog.

"Mom, no!" Bentley started toward Emerson, and Clarissa began crying.

"Bentley, stop right there. Clarissa, don't snivel. You're not ready to take care of a dog. Maybe when you're older, we'll talk about it."

Mrs. Serna pulled sunglasses from her purse. "Harold, take the man's money. Children, let's go home." She walked toward the door with her family in tow. "If we leave now, I can still make it to the symphony."

Mrs. Serna paused at the door, letting her family walk out first. She looked over her shoulder at Emerson and flashed a smile. Then she winked at him and closed the door behind her.

Lucky snuggled in Emerson's arms. *That mother wasn't so bad after all.* She wagged her tail and licked Emerson's face. *We talked for a while, you know. I told her I'll take care of you. I'll watch over you always and protect you. You're my boy. I will never, ever leave you.*

So she gave me back to you.

27

Grandpa Was Right

Emerson put Lucky down and hugged his grandfather's waist. "***Shi Cheii,*** thank you thank you thank you! You said you had a good feeling, but I was so scared. I didn't believe you, and I should have because you were right all the time."

Emerson let go and looked up at his grandfather. "You said maybe they wouldn't want her back, and look…." Emerson glanced down at Lucky. "No, they wanted her, all right. But Lucky didn't want them. She wanted me. And that lady, Mrs. Serna, she knew it. And I didn't even thank her."

Grandpa Charlie put his empty wallet back in his pocket. "If you see her again, you must remember to do so."

They said good-bye to Jolene and headed to the truck. Before Grandpa Charlie could start the engine,

Lucky jumped into his lap and began licking his chin.

"*Dooda. Dooda.*" Shaking his head, Grandpa Charlie shoved Lucky off his lap.

Emerson laughed. "*Shi Cheii,* she knows you helped. She's thanking you."

Grandpa Charlie shook his head. "The dog can thank me by staying out of trouble, *Shi Tsoi.*" He put the key in the ignition.

"Wait, *Shi Cheii,*" Emerson said, "Can we talk first? There's something I have to tell you. Actually, a lot I have to tell you."

His grandfather nodded and sat back in the seat.

Emerson placed Lucky on his lap and took a deep breath. "When I first got here, I was pretty mean to you, and I'm sorry. I said lots of horrible things to you. I thought if I made a lot of trouble, and you got mad enough, you'd send me home. But you didn't, not even when I forgot to close the lids." He looked at his grandfather. "I didn't do that on purpose, *Shi Cheii.* You were making me clean out the *dibe bighans,* and I was angry. I guess that's why I forgot."

His grandfather smiled. "I believe you."

"Then I found Lucky, and finally someone needed me. She wanted to be my friend when no one else did. I had to fight for her, but you let me keep her. That's when I began to like you." Emerson hugged Lucky to his chest.

"When Sam said her owners wanted her back, I panicked. *Shi Cheii,* I learned about ditches in school.

176

To stay out of them when it rains. And arroyos are big ditches. But I didn't think. I just wanted to run away with Lucky." He touched his grandfather's sleeve. "Lucky and me, we could have died in that arroyo, all because I didn't think." Tears welled up in his eyes, and he took off his glasses. "And you were there when I needed you. You saved my life." He sniffled and wiped his eyes with his sleeve.

Grandpa Charlie took the glasses and cleaned them with his bandana. Gently, he placed them back on his grandson's face.

Emerson took a gulp of air and looked at his grandfather. "*Shi Cheii,* I'm not that same kid I was when I got here. I've grown up. Even Lucky's grown up. She's learning to be a sheepdog. And I want to learn everything you said you'd teach me."

"Oh?" Grandpa Charlie lifted his eyebrows and smiled. "What did I say?"

"Well," Emerson counted on his fingers: "You said you'd teach me to build a fence, make fry bread and coffee, how to throw a lasso, how to find stuff in the desert to make soap. And you said you'd tell me all kinds of Navajo stories." He looked up at his grandfather. "Is that enough?"

Grandpa Charlie chuckled. "*Aoo, Shi Tsoi.* Does this mean you want to stay here after all? You don't want to go home?"

Before Emerson could answer, Grandpa Charlie's

cell phone rang in his pocket. He looked surprised, then pulled it out and punched the receive button. "Hello."

Grandpa Charlie's eyebrows drew together, listening. Then he said, *"Aoo.* He is right here." He handed the phone to Emerson. "It's your mother."

28
My Choice

Emerson grinned and put the phone to his ear. "Mom? It's really you?"

"Yes, honey, it's really me." Her voice sounded tiny over the phone. "I've missed you terribly."

"I miss you, too, Mom."

"I tried calling before, but I couldn't get through. Where are you now?"

"We're at the trading post. Mom, there's so much to tell you! I have a dog. Her name is Lucky, and you'll love her."

"A dog?" His mother's voice sounded doubtful.

"She's really little, Mom. A wiener dog and we're best friends."

He heard his mother laugh. "In that case, she can come home with you."

"And I'm learning a lot, too. Guess what? I can ride

181

a horse and herd sheep."

"Well, it sounds like you're finally having a little fun at sheep camp." She paused for a moment. "But Emerson, all of your messages sounded so sad. You said you were lonely and that you wanted to come home."

Emerson suddenly felt cold inside. He'd forgotten he left those messages. Now he didn't know what to say.

"I'm happy to have you come home to me," his mother continued. "I miss you, and Zach's mother said you could stay at their house while I'm in class. How soon do you want to come home? I'll work it out with Grandpa."

Emerson's heart plummeted to his stomach. "Uh, Mom, can you wait a minute?" His voice shook. "I need to talk to **Shi Cheii.**" Emerson dropped the phone in his lap. *It's what I wanted all along, to go home. Now I can.* He rubbed his forehead. *So what's wrong? I'm all jumbled up inside.*

Grandpa Charlie was looking out the side window. Emerson tugged on his shirtsleeve, and his grandfather faced him. *Grandpa's face looks sad. He never looked like that before.*

"Mom says I can go home," Emerson's voice wavered.

"Is that what you want, **Shi Tsoi?**"

Emerson looked down at the phone in his lap. He shook his head slowly. "I thought I did, but now I don't. I want to stay here with you." He looked up at his

182

grandfather. "You want me to stay, don't you?"

Grandpa Charlie pushed Emerson's hair off his forehead. "*Aoo, Shi Tsoi.* Very much."

Emerson grinned. Then he glanced at the cell in his lap and sighed. "Okay, then. I better tell Mom." Emerson's mouth trembled as he picked up the phone. "Mom?"

His mother's words were soft. "Honey, I heard what you and Grandpa said. I miss you, but I understand. Grandpa was a good father to me. He'll be a good grandfather to you." Then her voice brightened. "You know you can always change your mind. If you do, I'll come get you. If you don't, well, we'll have lots to talk about when summer is over."

"Okay, Mom." Now she sounded like she was starting to cry, and Emerson felt tears fill his eyes, too. "I love you, Mom."

"I love you, too. Let me talk to Grandpa now."

Emerson watched his grandfather's face as he nodded and said "*aoo*" to his daughter several times. Finally he said, "I will take good care of *Shi Tsoi,* Tina. *Hagoonee.*" He punched the "off" button and put the phone back in his pocket.

"Well, *Shi Tsoi,* it looks like we have the rest of the summer together, you and me." Grandpa Charlie backed the truck out of the parking lot and pulled onto the highway.

"You mean, you and me and Lucky. Don't forget her." Lucky bounced on Emerson's lap and poked her

183

head out the window.

His grandfather shook his head. "I would like to forget the dog, but I cannot. I bought her."

Emerson scratched his nose. "Yeah, you did. And you did it for me. Thirty dollars is a lot of money. I'll pay you back, *Shi Cheii.* I'll get a job when I go home and send the money to you. I promise."

Grandpa Charlie chuckled. "You will not have to get a job to pay me back."

"No?" Emerson turned to look at his grandfather. "How come?"

Grandpa Charlie's eyes twinkled. "Because, *Shi Tsoi,* you already have a job. For the rest of the summer, you will shovel out the *dibe bighans.*"

T'aa'akodi

(The End)

(For Now)

Don't Miss Emerson and Lucky in Their Next Adventure!

Danger at the Rodeo!   The gravel voiced man gripped Emerson's arm. "Whatta we got here? A spy? A sneak? What did you hear, kid?"

Emerson looked up. Two black eyes stared through holes in a hood. "I — I — I don't know," Emerson stuttered.

"Maybe you heard us, maybe you didn't. I can't take that chance." Gravel Voice leaned over and Emerson felt hot breath on his face. "What should I do with you so you don't talk?"

Emerson gasped and jerked his arm free. He bounded for the door but Gravel Voice grabbed his arm and yanked him back.

"Owww," Emerson cried out. Lucky snarled and lunged, but Bad Teeth jerked hard on her leash and kicked her. She yelped and scuttled away from him.

Seething with anger, Emerson pitched forward and kicked Bad Teeth in the shin. "I said, don't hurt her!"

Gravel Voice clamped both hands on Emerson's shoulders. "The kid just gave us the answer," he said to his friend. "We don't have to hurt him. We just have to hurt the dog…"

Coming soon, the further adventures of Emerson and Lucky in *Danger at the Rodeo*.

ABOUT THE AUTHOR

 Born in Yokohama, Japan, Karen grew up the eldest of six children in a military family. She majored in anthropology at the University of New Mexico, where she formed a lifelong interest in the Native American cultures of the Southwest. Karen shares her Albuquerque home with two miniature dachshunds, Xena and Mr. Bojangles. A retired hot-air balloon pilot, Karen currently spends her time working, writing and agility training Mr. Bo. *Stranded at Sheep Camp* is her first published book.

Made in the USA
San Bernardino, CA
19 September 2014